ANTSY DOES TIME

SCHOLASTIC INC.
New York Toronto London Auckland
Sydney Mexico City New Delhi Hong Kong

Neal Shusterman

ANTSY DOES TIME

ISBN 978-0-545-24221-9

12 11 10 9 8 7 6 5 4 3 2 1   10 11 12 13 14 15/0

Printed in the U.S.A.   40

First Scholastic printing, January 2010

Designed by Heather Wood

For Stephanie,
my editorial muse

"*When the parched land yields neither fruit nor flower, grain nor greens, a man will ask himself if the blame lies in the sheer weight of his transgressions, or is it just global warming?*"

—JOHN STEINBECK[*]

---

[*]NOT REALLY.

The Real Reason People Sit
Like Idiots Watching Parades

1 It was all my idea. The stupid ones usually are. Once in a while the genius ideas are mine, too. Not on purpose, though. You know what they say: if you put, like, fourteen thousand monkeys in front of computer keyboards for a hundred years, aside from a whole lot of dead monkeys, you'd end up with one masterpiece among the garbage. Then they'd start teaching it in schools to make you feel miserable, because if a monkey can write something brilliant, why can't you put five measly sentences together for a writing prompt?

This idea—I don't know whether it was a brilliant-monkey idea, or a stupid-Antsy idea, but it sure had power to change a whole lot of lives.

I called the idea "time shaving," which probably isn't what you think it is, so before you start whipping up time machines in your head, you need to listen to what it's all about. Nobody's going back in time to nuke Napoléon, or give Jesus a cell phone or anything. There's no time travel at all. People *are* going to die, though—and in strange and mysterious ways, too, if you're into that kind of thing.

Me, I was just trying to help a friend. I never meant for it to blow up like a giant Macy's Thanksgiving Day Parade balloon that gets taken away by the wind.

Which, by the way, is exactly how the whole thing began.

On Thanksgiving morning, my friends Howie and Ira and I were hanging out in my recreational attic. We used to have a recreational basement—you know, full of all our old cruddy furniture, a TV, and a big untouchable space in the corner that was going to be for a pool table when we could afford it in some distant *Star Trek*–like future. Then the basement gets this toxic mold, and we have to seal it off from the rest of the house, on account of the mold might escape and cause cancer, or brain damage, or take over the world. Even after the mold was cleaned out, my parents treated the basement like a radiation zone, uninhabitable for three generations.

So now we have a recreational attic, full of new old furniture, and space maybe for a Monopoly board instead of a pool table.

Anyway, Howie, Ira, and I were watching football that Thanksgiving morning, switching to the parade during commercials to make fun of the marching bands.

"Ooh! Ooh! Look at this one!" said Ira, with an expression that was a weird mix of joy and horror at the same time.

To the band's credit, they were playing an impressive rendition of "(I Can't Get No) Satisfaction," but anything cool about it was ruined by their pink-and-orange uniforms. Howie shakes his head. "As long as they dress like that, they're never getting any satisfaction."

"Antsy, don't you have a shirt like that?" asks Ira. My name's actually Anthony, but people have called me Antsy for so long, I oughta get it legally changed. I like it because there are so many Anthonys in the neighborhood, if some mother calls the name out a window, the stampede stops traffic. I'm the only Antsy, though—except for this one time a kid tried to steal it and call himself Antsy, so I had to start writing my name "Antsy®," and I threatened to punch him out for identity theft.

So anyway, about the shirt, although I hate to admit it, yeah, I do have a shirt in orange and pink, although it was a different shade of pink.

"Just because I have it doesn't mean I wear it," I tell Ira. The shirt was a birthday gift from my aunt Mona, who has no kids or common sense. I'll give you one guess how many times I've worn it since my fourteenth birthday.

"You think anyone's documented seizures from looking at that color combination?" asks Howie. "We should run some tests."

"Great. I'll get my shirt, you can stare at it for six hours, and we'll see if you go into convulsions."

Howie seriously considers this. "Can I break for meals?"

Let me try to explain Howie to you. You know that annoying automated customer-service voice on the phone that wastes your time before making you hold for a real person? Well, Howie's the music on hold. It's not that Howie's dumb—he's got a fertile mind when it comes to analytical stuff like math—but his imagination is a cold winter in Antarctica where the penguins never learned to swim.

On TV, the band had almost passed, and one of the giant parade balloons could be seen in the distance. This one was the classic cartoon *Roadkyll Raccoon*, complete with that infamous tire track down his back, the size of a monster-truck tread. We were about to turn the TV back to football, but then Ira noticed something.

"Is it my imagination, or is Roadkyll on the warpath?"

Sure enough, Roadkyll is kicking and bucking like he's Godzilla trying to take out Tokyo. Then this huge gust of wind rips off the band members' hats, and when the gust reaches Roadkyll, he kind of peels himself off the street, and heads to the skies. Most of the balloon handlers have the good sense to let go, except for three morons who decide to go up with the ship.

Suddenly this is more interesting than the game.

Howie sighs. "I've said it before, I'll say it again. Helium kills."

The cameras were no longer watching the parade—they're all aimed at the airborne raccoon as it rises in an updraft along the side of the Empire State Building, with the three balloon wranglers clinging like circus acrobats. Then, just as it looks like Roadkyll might be headed for the moon, he gets snagged on top of the Empire State Building and punctures. In less than a minute the balloon has totally deflated over the spire, covering the top of the Empire State Building in rubber coonskin and stranding the three danglers, who hang from their ropes for their lives.

I was the first one out of my seat.

"Let's go," I said, because there are some events in life that are better experienced in person than viewed on TV.

We took the subway into Manhattan—usually a crowded ride from our little corner of Brooklyn, but since it was Thanksgiving, the trains were mostly empty, except for others like ourselves who were on their way to the Empire State Building to watch history in the making.

Ira, who has an intense and questionable relationship with his video camera, was lovingly cleaning the lens as he prepared to record today's event for future generations. Howie was reading *Of Mice and Men,* which we all had to read for English. It's a book the teachers use to trick us—because it's really thin, but it's like, deep, so you gotta read it twice.

Across from us in the train was Gunnar Ümlaut—a kid who moved here from Sweden when we were all in elementary school. Gunnar's got long blond hair he makes no excuse for, and a resigned look of Scandinavian despair that melts girls in his path. And if that doesn't work, the slight accent he puts on when he's around girls does the job. Never mind that he's been living in Brooklyn since he was six. Not that I'm jealous or anything—I admire a guy who uses what he's got.

"Hi, Gunnar," I said. "Where you headed?"

"Where else? The Roadkyll debacle."

"Excellent," I said, and filed the word "debacle" in the special place I reserve for words I will never know the meaning of.

So Gunnar's sitting there, all slouched and casual, his arms across seats on either side like maybe there's a couple of invisible girls there. (Don't get me started on invisible. Long story.) Then he takes one look at Howie's book and says, "The dumb guy dies at the end."

Howie looks up at Gunnar, heaves a heavy sigh that can only

come from a lifetime of ruined endings, and closes the book. I snicker, which just irritates Howie even more.

"Thanks, Gunnar." Howie sneers. "Any more spoilers you care to share with us?"

"Yeah," says Gunnar. "Rosebud's a sled, the spider dies after the fair, and the Planet of the Apes is actually Earth in the distant future." He doesn't smile when he says it. Gunnar never smiles. I think girls must like that, too.

By the time we got off at Thirty-fourth Street, the parade crowd had all gravitated to the Empire State Building, hoping to experience the thrill of watching someone they don't know plunge to his death.

"If they don't survive," said Gunnar, "it's our responsibility to witness it. As Winston Churchill once said, *'An untimely end witnessed, gives life deeper meaning.'*"

Gunnar always talks like that—all serious, as if even stupidity has a point.

All around us the police are screaming at the crowds, one hand on their batons, saying things like, "Don't make me use this!"

Up above, the Empire State Building was still wearing a coonskin hat, and the three unfortunate balloon handlers were exactly where they were when we left home—still clinging on to their ropes. Ira handed me the camera, which had a 500X zoom, just in case I wanted to examine one of the guy's nose hairs.

It was hard to hold the camera steady when it was zoomed in, but once I did, I could see firefighters and police inside the Empire State Building, trying to reach the men through the windows. They weren't having much luck. Word in the crowd was that a rescue helicopter was on its way.

One guy had managed to tie the rope around his waist and was swinging toward the windows, but the rescuers couldn't get a grip on him. The second guy clung to the rope and also had it hooked around his feet, probably thanking the New York public school system for forcing him to learn how to do this in gym class. The third guy was the worst off. He was dangling from a stick at the end of his rope, holding on with both hands like a flying trapeze once it stops flying.

"Hey, I wanna look, too!"

Howie grabs the camera from me, and that's just fine, because I was starting to get a bad feeling in the pit of my stomach. Suddenly I started to wonder what had possessed me to come down here at all.

"How much you wanna bet those guys write a book about this?" says Howie. It seems Howie assumes they're all going to survive.

All the while, Gunnar just stood there quietly, his eyes cast heavenward toward the human drama, with a solemn expression on his face. He caught me watching him.

"For the past few months I've been coming to disasters," Gunnar tells me.

"Why?"

Gunnar shrugs as if it's nothing, but I can tell there's more to it. "I find them . . . compelling."

Coming from anyone else, this would be like a serial-killer warning sign, but from Gunnar it didn't seem weird at all, it just seemed like some profound Scandinavian thing—like all those foreign movies where everyone dies, including the director, the cameraman, and half the audience.

Gunnar shakes his head sadly as he watches the souls up above. "So fragile . . ." he says.

"What," says Howie, "balloons?"

"No, human life, you idiot," I tell him. For an instant I caught a hint of what actually might have been a smile on Gunnar's face. Maybe because I said what he was thinking.

There's applause all around us, and when I look up, I can see the swinging man has finally been caught by a cop, and he's hauled through the window. The helicopter has arrived with a guy tethered to a rope like an action hero, to go after the trapeze dangler. The crowd watches in a silence you rarely hear in a city. It takes a few hair-raising minutes, but the guy is rescued and hauled away by the helicopter. Now only one dangler remains. This is the guy who seemed calmest of all; the guy who had it all under control. The guy who suddenly slips, and plunges.

A singular gasp from the audience.

"No way!" says Ira, his eye glued to his camera.

The guy falls. He falls forever. He doesn't even spin his arms—it's like he's already accepted his fate. And suddenly I find I can't watch it. I snap my eyes away, looking anywhere else. My shoes, other people's shoes, the manhole cover beneath me.

I never heard him hit. I'm thankful that I didn't. Yeah, it was my idea to come here, but when it comes right down to it, I know there are some things you just shouldn't watch. That's when I saw Gunnar—for all his talk about witnessing disaster, he was looking away, too. Not just looking away, but grimacing and covering his eyes.

The gasps from the crowd have turned to groans of self-loathing as people suddenly realize this wasn't about entertainment. Even Howie and Ira are looking kind of ill.

"Let's get out of here before the subway gets packed," I tell them, trying to sound less choked up than I really am—but if I'm a little queasy, it's nothing compared to Gunnar. He was so pale I thought he might pass out. He even stumbles a little bit. I grab his arm to keep him steady. "Hey . . . Hey, you okay?"

"Yeah," he says. "I'm fine. It's nothing. Just a part of the illness."

I looked at him, not quite sure I heard him right. "Illness?"

"Yes. Pulmonary Monoxic Systemia." And then he says, "I only have six months to live."

Heaven, Hockey, and
the Ice Water of Despair

2 The idea of dying never appealed to me much. Even when I was a kid, watching the *Adventures of Roadkyll Raccoon and Darren Headlightz*, I always found it suspicious the way Roadkyll got flattened at the end of each cartoon and yet was back for more in the next episode. It didn't mesh with any reality I knew. According to the way I was raised, there are really just a few possibilities of what happens to you in the hereafter.

Option one: It turns out you're less of a miserable person than you thought you were, and you go to heaven.

Option two: You're not quite the wonderful person you thought you were, and you go to the other place that people these days spell with double hockey sticks, which, by the way, doesn't make much sense, because that's the only sport they can't play down there unless they're skating on boiling water instead of ice, but it ain't gonna happen, because all the walk-on-water types'll be up in heaven.

I did a report on heaven for Sunday school once, so I know all about it. In heaven, you're with your dead relatives, it's always sunny, and everyone's got nice views—no one's looking at a disgusting landfill or anything. I gotta tell you, though, if I gotta spend eternity with all my relatives, everybody hugging and walking with God and stuff, I'll go crazy. It sounds like my cousin Gina's wedding before people got drunk. I hope God don't mind me saying so, but it all sounds very hockey-stickish to me.

As for the place down under, the girl who did her report on it got all her information from horror movies, so, aside from really good special effects, her version is highly suspect. Supposedly there are like nine levels, and each one is worse than the last. Imagine a barbecue where *you're* sizzling on the grill— but it's not accidental like my dad last summer. And the thing about it is, you cook like one of them Costco roasts that's somehow thicker than an entire cow, so no matter how long you sit there, you're still rare in the middle for all eternity.

My mother, who I'm sure gives advice to God since she gives it to everyone else, says the fire talk is just to scare people. In reality, it's cold and lonely. Eternal boredom—which sounds right, because that's worse than the roasting version. At least when you're burning, you've got something to occupy your mind.

There is a third option, called Purgatory, which is a kinder, gentler version of the place down under. Purgatory is God's version of a time-out—temporary flames of woe. I find this idea most appealing, although to be honest, it all bugs me a little. I mean, God loves us and is supposed to be the perfect parent, right? So what if a parent came up to their kid and said, "I love you, but I'm going to have to punish you by roasting you over flames of woe, and it's really going to hurt." Social Services would not look kindly upon this, and we could all end up in foster care.

I figure Hell and Purgatory are like those parental threats— you know, like, "Tease your sister one more time, and I swear I'll kill you," or "Commit one more mortal sin, and so help me, I will roast you over eternal flames, young man."

Call me weird, but I find that comforting. It means that God really does love us, He's just ticked off.

Still, none of that was comforting when it came to Gunnar Ümlaut. The thought of someone I know dying, who wasn't old and dying already, really bothered me. It made me wish I knew Gunnar better, but then if I did, I'd be really sad now, so why would I want that, and should I feel guilty for not wanting it? The whole thing reeked of me having to feel guilty for something, and I hate that feeling.

Nobody talked much on the return trip from the Roadkyll Raccoon incident. Between what we witnessed and what Gunnar had told me, there just wasn't much anyone wanted to say. We talked about the football games we were missing, and school stuff, but mostly we looked at subway advertisements and out the windows so we wouldn't have to look at one another. I wondered if Howie and Ira had heard what Gunnar had told me, but didn't want to ask.

"See ya," was all anyone said when we got off the train. Howie, Ira, and Gunnar all went off to their Thanksgiving meals, and I went home to find a note from my parents, with exclamation points and underlines, telling me to be at the restaurant <u>ON TIME!!!</u>

My dad runs a French/Italian fusion restaurant called *Paris, Capisce?* He didn't always do this. He used to have an office job with a plastics company, but he lost it because of me. That's okay, though, because he got the restaurant because of me as well. It's a long story from the weird world of Old Man Crawley. If you've heard of him, and who hasn't, you'll know it's a story best kept at ten-foot-pole distance. Anyway, it all worked out in the end, because running a restaurant is what my dad always dreamed of doing.

We all quickly found out, however, that when you have a restaurant, you don't run it, it runs you. We all got sucked in. Mom fills in when there aren't enough waitresses, I'm constantly on call to bus tables, and my little sister Christina folds napkins into animal shapes. Only my older brother Frankie gets out of it, on account of he's in college, and when he's home, he thinks he's too good to work in a restaurant.

My particular skill is the pouring of water.

Don't laugh—it's a real skill. I can pour from any height and never miss the glass. People applaud.

Thanksgiving, we all knew, was going to be the big test. Not just of the restaurant, but of our family. See, Thanksgiving has always been big with us, on account of we got this massive extended family of aunts, uncles, cousins, and people I barely know who have various body parts resembling mine. That's what family is. But these days more and more people eat out on Thanksgiving, so Dad decided to offer a special

Thanksgiving meal at *Paris, Capisce?* instead of the usual big family meal at our house. That got the relatives all bent out of shape. We told them we're doing Thanksgiving at home one day late, but they flatly refused to postpone the holiday. Now we're family outcasts, at least until Christmas, when everyone will, in theory, kiss and make up. Dad knows better than to keep the restaurant open on Christmas, because Mom told him if he does, he'd better set up a cot in the back room, because that's where he'll be sleeping for a while. Mom says things like this very directly, because my father is not good with subtle hints.

As for Thanksgiving, Mom was very direct with the rest of us as well. "None of youse are allowed to eat any turkey this Thursday, got it? As far as you're concerned, Thanksgiving is on Friday."

"Do turkey hot dogs count?" I asked, because no direct order from my mother was complete unless I found a way around it. Not that I had plans to eat turkey hot dogs, but it's the principle of the thing. Mom's response was a look that probably wilted the lettuce in the refrigerator.

Part of her laying down of the law was that we weren't allowed to have a turkeyless Thanksgiving at friends' houses either—because if we did, our own family Thanksgiving would feel like an afterthought. I didn't think I'd really mind, but right now I didn't want to be alone with my thoughts. I was still feeling funny about the dead raccoon wrangler, and Gunnar's terminal confession, but it was still a while until Mom and Dad wanted me at the restaurant.

I tried to watch some football, and took to petting Ichabod, our cat, who was ninety-one in dog years, although I don't know what that means to a cat. But even Ichabod knew I was distracted, so he went off to watch Christina's hamsters run endlessly on their wheel. I suppose that's the feline equivalent of going to the market and watching the rotisserie chicken, which is how my mom entertained me at the market when I was little.

In the end, I left early, and took a long, wandering path to the restaurant. As I passed our local skate park, I saw one lonely soul sitting outside by the padlocked gate. I knew the kid, but not his name—only his nickname. He used to wear a shirt that said SKATERDUDE, but the E peeled off, and from that moment on he was eternally "Skaterdud." Like my nickname, he had grown into it, and everyone agreed it suited him to a tee. He was lanky with massively matted red hair, pink spots all over his joints from old peeled scabs, and eyes that you'd swear were looking into alternate dimensions, not all of them sane. God help the poor parents who see Skaterdud waiting at the door for their daughter on prom night.

"Hey, Dud," I said as I approached.

"Hey." He gave me his special eight-part handshake, and wouldn't continue the conversation until I got it right.

"So, no turkey?" I asked.

He smirked. "I ain't gonna miss not eatin' no dead bird, am I?"

Skaterdud had his own language all full of double, triple, and sometimes quadruple negatives, so you never really knew if he meant what he said, or the opposite.

"So . . . you're a vegan?" I asked.

"Naah." He patted his stomach. "Ate the dead bird early. What about you?"

I shrugged, not wanting to get into it. "This year we're celebrating Chinese Thanksgiving."

He raised his eyebrows knowingly. "Year of the Goat. Gotta love it."

"So," I asked, "isn't the skate park closed for the winter? What, are you gonna sit here and wait till it reopens in the spring?"

He shook his head. "Unibrow said he'd come down and open it for me today. But I don't see no Unibrow, do you?"

I sat down and leaned against the fence, figuring that chatting with Skaterdud was as good a mental distraction as any. Kind of like playing Minesweeper with a human being. We talked about school, and I was amazed at how the Dud knew more details about his teachers' personal lives than he did about any given subject. We talked about his lipring, and how he got it to stop him from biting his nails. I nodded like I understood how the two things were related. And then we talked about Gunnar. I told him about Gunnar's imminent death, and he looked down, picking at a peeling skull sticker on his helmet.

"That chews the churro, man," said Skaterdud. "But ya can't do nothin' about no bad freakin' luck, right? Everybody's got a song on the fat lady's list." Then he thought for a second. "Of course I ain't got no worries, 'cause I know exactly when I'm doing the dirt dance."

"Whaddaya mean?"

"Oh, yeah," said the Dud. "I know exactly when I'm croaking. A fortune-teller told me. She said I'm dying when I'm forty-nine by falling off the deck of an aircraft carrier."

"No way!"

"Yeah. That's how come I'm joining the navy. Because how screwed would it be to fall off an aircraft carrier when you're not even supposed to be there?"

Then he stood up and hurled his skateboard over the fence. "Enough of this noise." He climbed the fence with the skill of a gecko, then looked back to me from the other side. "You wanna come over? I'll teach you stuff the other kids gotta break bones to learn."

"Maybe another time. Nice talkin'."

"Yeah," he says, and heads off. In a moment he disappears over the concrete lip, and I can hear him zipping in and out of concrete ramps that were slick with patches of ice, not caring how dangerous it might be, because he's so sure he's safe for another thirty-four years.

I got to the restaurant on time, but I felt like I was late because everything was in full swing. Since most of our Thanksgiving reservations were for later in the afternoon, my dad didn't expect it to get crowded until around two, and he didn't want me hanging around with nothing to do, since that was "a recipe for disaster." But they hadn't counted on all the holiday walk-ins. There weren't enough walk-ins to fill the restaurant, but it sure was enough to make my father run around like a maniac, which made my mother do the same. Only my sister Christina was calm as she folded napkins into swans and unicorns, and placed them at each table. Dad had given most of his staff Thanksgiving off, since he's such a pushover, so that meant more work for the family.

Just watching my dad work is enough to exhaust you. He's

like the plate spinner at the circus—he's got to keep everything going, see everything at once. Maybe it's because he's overcompensating. He doesn't have any formal training in running a restaurant, just a head full of great recipes, and a rich, cranky old business partner willing to give him a chance.

"Old Man Crawley is a very hard man to please," my dad had told me. Having worked for Crawley myself last year—as the walker of his many dogs, among other things—I knew more than anyone how hard he was to please. Used to be my dad worked long hours in a job that he hated. Now he works longer hours in a job that he loves, but he seems just as brain-dead at the end of the day.

Anyway, when Dad saw me come in, he took a moment out of the mania to give me a hug, and a mini neck massage.

"Water-pouring muscles all ready?" he asked. It was a bit of an inside joke, on account of my shoulder muscles used to lock into a shrug after my first few days as a busboy. Who knew pouring water could be so strenuous.

"Yeah," I told him.

"Good," he said. "'Cause one of these days they're gonna make 'The Water Pour' an Olympic event, and I expect to see nothing but gold." He handed me an apron, slapped me on the back, then went back to work. I really like being around my dad early in the day, before the stress turns him into what we in our family like to call "Darth Menu."

Pretty soon my mind was occupied pouring water and taking away dirty plates, but thoughts of the doomed raccoon guy and Gunnar never entirely faded into the background.

By 6 P.M., we were already into our second seating, and I

was a bit grumpy, because I kept taking away all these plates of food, but I couldn't eat any of it myself. Both Mom and Dad had come up with great Thanksgiving recipes that fit the French/Italian theme of the restaurant. Pumpkin Parmesan Quiche, and Turkey Rollatini au Vin—stuff like that. I got so hungry I would pick at some of the leftovers I took away from the tables, and that got me a whack on the head from Mom. While the skeleton crew of regular staff had breaks every few hours, family members were slaves today, and I resented it.

So I'm moving plates and pouring water, and I can't help thinking that here are all these people stuffing their fat faces, while some poor slob died simply because he got stuck holding on to a balloon—and then there was Gunnar. How could these people eat when he was suffering from pulmo-whachamacallit?

That's when it happened. The glass of ice water I was pouring overflowed. The moment I realized it, I jerked the pitcher back, but that only succeeded in sloshing ice cubes onto the woman's dinner plate.

"Oops!" Then I reached onto her plate like an idiot and started plucking ice cubes out of her Garlique Yam Puree with my bare fingers.

"ANTSY!"

Like I said, my dad saw everything all at once in the restaurant, and I had been caught red-handed—or orange-handed, as it were.

"What do you think you're doing?!"

"I . . . I spilled. I was just—"

"It's all right," said the woman. "No harm done."

But she was wrong about that. "We'll get you a new plate right away," my father said. "I'm sorry for the trouble. Your meal is on the house."

By now my mom and the other waitress had come over to help clean up the spill. Dad handed me the plate of food and pointed to the kitchen. "Take this away and wait for me."

He apologized to the woman again, and maybe even a third time. I don't know because I was already in the kitchen, cleaning off the plate and awaiting judgment. It wasn't long in coming. In just a few seconds, he was there, all fire and brimstone. I could tell the day had already burned him out, and he had gone over to the Dark Side.

"I can't believe what you did in there! Where is your head?"

"Dad, it was just a spill! I said I was sorry!"

"Just a spill? Your fingers were in her food! Do you have any idea how many health codes you broke?"

I'll admit that I deserved to be reprimanded, but he was out of control.

That's when Mom poked her head in, and said in a whisper that was louder than most people scream, "Will you keep it down? The whole restaurant can hear you!"

But Dad was a runaway train. "How could you be so irresponsible?"

"Well, maybe I have something else on my mind!"

"No! When you're here, you can't have *anything* else on your mind!"

"Why don't you just fire me?" I snapped. "Oh, that's right, you can't fire me—because I don't actually *work* here, do I?"

"You know what, Antsy? Just go home."

"Fine, I will!" And for my parting shot, I dipped my finger in the big pot of Garlique Yam Puree, and licked it off.

It was long after dark now, and the walk home was freezing. I thought my brother Frankie might be at home to keep me company, since he was back from Binghamton for the weekend, but he was off with friends, so I had nothing to do but hang out and stew.

The phone rang at about eight-thirty. On the other end was Old Man Crawley, who owned more of my father's restaurant than my father did. Getting a call from Crawley was worse than getting chewed out by my dad.

"I understand service was sloppy tonight," Crawley said.

"Did my father tell you that?"

"I haven't spoken with your father. I sent an observer to eat at the restaurant."

"You sent a spy to your own restaurant?"

"Espionage is a common business practice."

"Against yourself?"

"Apparently it was warranted."

I sighed. Old Man Crawley had more eyes in more places than anyone I knew. I wouldn't be surprised if right now he told me to stop picking my nose.

In case you've been living under a rock, I oughta tell you a little bit about Old Man Crawley, or "Creepy Crawley," as all the little kids call him. The guy's a legend in Brooklyn— the kind you really don't believe until you actually meet him, but by then it's too late to run. He's very rich, very selfish, and generally mean. He's the kind of guy who'd hand out vomit-inducing candy on Halloween, and then sell Pepto-Bismol across the street at jacked-up prices.

I'm one of the few people who actually knows him, on account of he's mostly a hermit. He used to be entirely a hermit, until he hired me to walk his dogs and to date his granddaughter, Lexie, who's blind, but has managed to make her blindness seem like a mere technicality. Pretty soon dating her stopped being a job, and it became real, much to Old Man Crawley's disgust. There was this one time Lexie and I kidnapped Crawley, and forced him to see the outside world. He liked it so much he now has us kidnap him on a regular basis.

The weird thing is that I kind of like him. Maybe it's because I understand him—or maybe it's because I'm the only person who can call him a nasty old fart to his face and get away with it. I can't quite say that Crawley and I are friends, but he dislikes me less than he dislikes most other people. Still, with Crawley, the line between tolerance and disgust is very thin.

"If you give me the details of tonight's incident, maybe I won't have to ask your father about it," Crawley said.

There was no sense in lying to Old Man Crawley. No sense sugarcoating it either, so I told it to him as plainly, and as simply, as I could. "I spilled some water, and plucked ice cubes off some woman's plate, so my father had to give her a free meal. Then he sent me home."

A long silence on the other end. I could hear dogs barking in the background, and then Crawley said, "I am amazed, Anthony, by your continuing ability to disappoint me." And then he hung up without as much as a good-bye.

———

Mom came home at about ten that night, with Christina practically asleep in her arms. I knew Dad wouldn't be home until past midnight. It was like that all the time, since he opened the restaurant. On this particular night, though, I didn't mind.

My mom came into my room once she got Christina off to bed. "You gotta understand, Antsy, your father's under a lot of pressure."

"Yeah, well, he doesn't have to take it out on me."

"He doesn't mean to."

"Blah, blah, blah."

She sat on the edge of my bed. "The restaurant's not doing as well as he would like. Mr. Crawley keeps threatening to pull the plug."

I sat up, and before she could launch into the Top Ten Reasons Why I Should Cut My Father Some Slack, I said, "I get it, okay? But just because I get it doesn't mean I gotta like it."

She patted my leg, then left, satisfied.

When Dad got home around midnight, he made a point to stop by my room. Even before he spoke, I could tell that Darth Menu had left the building.

"Things good?" he asked.

Since there was no short answer, I just said, "Things are things."

"So," he asked, with a crooked little smile. "Did you at least like the Garlique Yam Puree?"

This, I knew, was an apology.

"Yeah, it was good," I said. "All your stuff is good."

This, he knew, was me accepting his apology.

"Good night, Antsy."

After he left, I turned off my TV and tried to get to sleep. As I lay there, at the place where your thoughts start to break apart and stop making sense, the day's events began to swim into a soup of raccoon, ice water, and terminal illness. Like Gunnar had said, life is a fragile thing. One moment you could be marching happily in a parade, the next you're hanging from the Empire State Building. Sometimes it's because of the choices you make, or sometimes you're just careless—but most of the time it's just dumb luck—and in my experience few things are dumber than luck, except for maybe Wendell Tiggor, whose brain cells communicate by smoke signal.

Luck was about to take some pretty weird bounces, though. It never occurred to me how something as simple as a pitcher of ice water could change a person's life . . . or how a single piece of paper could change the course of an incurable disease.

Why "NeuroToxin" Is Now My
Favorite Word in the English Language

3 Pulmonary Monoxic Systemia. Very rare. Very fatal. Basically the body, which is supposed to turn oxygen into carbon dioxide, turns it into carbon monoxide instead—the stuff in car exhaust that kills you if you breathe it long enough. In other words, when you've got Pulmonary Monoxic Systemia, your own body fails the smog check, and you're eventually poisoned by the very air you breathe. I think I'd rather fall from a giant inflatable raccoon.

There are several different ways to respond when you find out that someone you know has something weird and incurable. Your response all depends on the type of person you are. There are basically three types.

Type One: The "I-didn't-hear-that" people. These are the ones who just go on with life, pretending that nothing is wrong. These are the people who would be sitting in Starbucks during an alien invasion, arguing the virtues of Splenda over Equal. You know this person. We all do.

Type Two: The "not-in-my-airspace" people. These are the ones who believe that everything is somehow contagious and would probably start taking antibiotics if their computer got a virus. These people would do everything within their power to avoid the terminally ill person, and then say, "I wish we had more time with him," once the farm had been bought.

Type Three: The "I-can-fix-this" people. These people, against all logic, believe they can change the course of mighty rivers with their bare hands, even thought they can't swim, and so usually end up drowning.

I come from a family of drowners.

I guess I follow in the family tradition—because even though I couldn't even pronounce the illness that Gunnar had, I was convinced that I could somehow help him live longer. By the time I went back to school on Monday, I had already decided that I wanted to do something Meaningful for him. I wasn't sure what it would be, only that it would be Meaningful. Now keep in mind this was before I met Kjersten, so my intentions weren't selfish yet. I was being what they call "altruistic," which means doing good deeds for no sensible reason—and having no sensible reason for doing things is kind of where I live.

I knew I'd be on my own in figuring this one out—or at least I wasn't going to ask for help from my family. Talking to Dad about it was out of the question, because all of his mental wall space was covered with restaurant reservations. I couldn't tell my mom, because the second I did, she'd get that pained expression on her face and be on my case about praying for Gunnar. Not that I wouldn't pray for Gunnar, but I probably would be strategic about it. I wouldn't do it until he was on his deathbed, because the way I see it, praying is like trying to win an Academy Award; you don't want to come out praying too early, or you get forgotten when it's time for the nominations.

I considered telling Frankie or Christina, but Frankie would just try to top it by telling me all the people *he* knew who died. As for Christina, traumatizing her with this was a bit different from telling her our basement was sealed off because of the zombies. Besides, who goes to their younger sister for advice? She does have a spiritual streak, though, I'll admit that. In fact, lately I've found her sitting in her room, in lotus position, trying to levitate. She read somewhere that monks in the Himalayas have special spiritual mantras they repeat over and over that will make them float in midair. I'm open to all possibilities, but I told Christina that her mantra of "Ama Gonna Levitato" sounded more Harry Potter than Himalaya.

No, this whole thing needed to fly under my family's radar for a while.

Few things got by our school radar, however. It could have been Howie or Ira who overheard Gunnar at the Empire State Building—or maybe Gunnar had been selectively confiding in other kids as well. Whatever the reason, Gunnar's life-span issue was all the whisper around school on Monday.

That was the day we had to sign up for John Steinbeck lit circles in English class. Apparently *Of Mice and Men* was just a prelude to a whole lot of reading. I showed up a few minutes late, and all the short books like *The Red Pony* were gone, leaving monsters like *The Grapes of Wrath* and *East of Eden*.

Gunnar and I were in English together, and I noticed that he was in the *Grapes of Wrath* group. The *Cannery Row* group consisted of Wendell Tiggor and the tiggorhoids—which is what we called all the human moths that fluttered around Tiggor's dim bulb. I make it a habit never to join any group where I'm the smartest member, so I put my name under Gunnar's and prayed that *The Grapes of Wrath* wasn't as deep as it was long. If nothing else, it would give me a chance to get to know Gunnar better, and figure out what Meaningful thing I could do for him.

After class he came up to me. "So I see we're both in the Group of Wrath," he said. "Why don't you come over after school—I've got the movie on DVD."

It was pretty bad timing, because just then Mrs. Casey, our English teacher, was passing by. "That's cheating, Mr. Ümlaut," she said.

"No," I offered, without missing a beat. "It's research."

She raised an eyebrow as she considered this. "In that case, I'm assigning you both to compare and contrast the book with the movie." Then she struts off, very pleased with herself.

Gunnar sighed. "Sorry about that."

I leaned closer to him and whispered, "It's okay—I think my brother's got the Cliff's Notes."

And from the far end of the hall Mrs. Casey yells back, "Don't even think about it!"

Going over to someone's house you barely know is always an adventure of strange smells, strange sights, and strange dogs that will either yap at you or sniff places you'd rather not be sniffed. But there's interesting things at unexplored homes as well, like a giant tank of Chinese water dragons, or a home theater better than the multiplex, or a goddess answering the door.

In the Ümlauts' case, it was choice number three: the goddess. Her name was Kjersten, pronounced "Kirsten" (the *j* is silent—don't ask me how that's possible) and she was the last person I expected to see at Gunnar's house. Kjersten is a junior, and exists on a plane high above us mere mortals—and not just because of her height. She doesn't fit the mold of your typical beautiful girl. She's not a cheerleader, she's not part of the popular crowd—in fact, the popular crowd hates her, because Kjersten's very presence points out to them how pitiful they really are. She is a straight-A student, rules the debate team, is on the tennis team, is practically six feet tall, and as for other parts of her, well, let's just say that the lettering on her T-shirt is like one of those movies in 3-D.

"Hi, Antsy."

My response was a perfect imitation of Porky Pig. "Ibbidi-bibbiby-dibbity . . ." The fact that Kjersten even knew I existed was too much information for me to process.

She gave a little laugh. "NeuroToxin," she said.

"Huh?"

"You were looking at my shirt." She pointed to the logo on her chest. "It's the band NeuroToxin—I got it at their concert last month."

"Yeah, yeah, right." To be honest, in spite of where my eyes were staring, my brain had turned everything between her neck and her navel into that digital blur they put up on TV when they don't want you to see something. Her shirt could have had the answers to tomorrow's math test on it and I wouldn't have known.

"What are you doing here?" I said, like a perfect imbecile.

She gave me a funny look. "Where else would I be? I live here."

"Why do you live with the Ümlauts?"

She laughed again. "Uh . . . maybe because I *am* an Ümlaut?"

With my brain somewhere between here and Jupiter, I was only now catching on. "So you're Gunnar's sister?"

"Last I checked."

The concept that Kjersten could be the sister of someone I actually knew had never occurred to me. I suppressed the urge to do another Porky Pig, swallowed, and said, "Can I come in, please?"

"Sure thing." Then she called to Gunnar, letting him know that I was here. I shivered when she said my name again, and hoped she hadn't seen.

There was no response from Gunnar—the only thing I heard was a faint, high-pitched banging sound.

"He's out back working on that *thing*," Kjersten said. "Just go on through the kitchen and out the back door."

I thanked her, tried not to stare at any part of her whatsoever, and went into the house. As I passed through the kitchen I saw their mother—a woman who looked like an older, plumper version of Kjersten.

"Hello!" she said when she saw me, looking up from some vegetables she was cleaning in the sink. "You must be a friend of Gunnar's. Will you stay for dinner?" Her accent was much heavier than I expected it to be, considering Gunnar and Kjersten barely had any accent at all.

Dinner? I thought. That would mean I'd be at the same dinner table with Kjersten, and the moment I thought that, my own mother's voice intruded into my head, telling me that I used utensils like an orangutang. Whenever Mom said that, I would respond by telling her that orangutan had no *g* at the end and then go on shoveling food into my mouth like a lower primate. My eating habits didn't matter with my last girlfriend, Lexie, on account of she's blind. She would just get mad when I scraped the fork against my teeth, so as long as I ate quietly, I could be as apelike as I pleased.

Now, thanks to my own stubbornness, I had no practice in fine dining skills. Kjersten would take one look at the way I held my knife and fork, would burst out laughing, and share the information with whatever higher life-forms she communed with.

I knew if I dwelt on this much longer, I would either talk myself out of it or my head would explode, so I said, "Sure, I'll stay for dinner." I'd deal with the consequences later.

"Antsy, is that you?" Gunnar called from the backyard, where the loud tapping sound was coming from.

"Maybe," Mrs. Ümlaut said quietly, "you shall get him away from that *thing* he works on."

Gunnar was, indeed, working on a thing. I wondered at first if it was something for our *Grapes of Wrath* project. It was a stone sculpture. Granite or marble, I guessed. He was tapping away at it with a hammer and chisel. He hadn't gotten too far, because the block of stone was still pretty square. "Hi, Gunnar," I said. "I didn't know you were an artist."

"Neither did I."

He continued his tapping. There were uneven letters toward the edge of the block. *G-U-N.* He was already working on the second *N.* I laughed. "You gotta make the sculpture before you sign it, Gunnar."

"It's not that kind of sculpture."

It took me a moment more until I got the big picture, and the moment I realized just what Gunnar was doing, I blurted out one of those words my mother smacks me for.

Gunnar was carving his own tombstone.

"Gunnar . . . that's just . . . *wrong.*"

He stood back to admire his work. "Well, the letters aren't exactly even, but that will add to the overall effect."

"That's not what I mean."

He looked at me, read what must have been a pretty unpleasant expression on my face, and said, "You're just like my parents. You have an unhealthy attitude. Did you know that in ancient Egypt the Pharaohs began planning their own tombs when they were still young?"

"Yeah, but you're Swedish," I reminded him. "There aren't any pyramids in Sweden."

He finished off the second *N.* "That's only because Vikings weren't good with stone."

I found myself involuntarily looking around for an escape route, and wondered if maybe I was a "not-in-my-airspace" type after all.

Then Gunnar starts launching into all this talk about death throughout history, and how people in Borneo put their departed loved ones in big ceramic pots and keep them in the living room, which is worse than anything I've told my sister about our basement. So I'm getting all nauseous and stuff, and his mother calls out, "Dinner's ready," and I pray to God she's not serving out of a Crock-Pot.

"Borrowed time, Antsy," he said. "I'm living on borrowed time."

It annoyed me, because he wasn't living on borrowed time— he was living on his own time, at least for six months, and I could think of better things to do with that time than carving a tombstone.

"Will you just shut up!" I told him.

He looked at me, hurt. "I thought you of all people would understand."

"Whaddaya mean 'me of all people'? Do you know something I don't?"

We both looked away. He said, "When that guy . . . the other day . . . you know . . . when he fell from Roadkyll Raccoon . . . everyone else was staring like it was some show, but you and I . . . we had respect enough to look away. So I thought you'd have respect for me, too." He glanced at the unfinished gravestone before him. "And respect for this."

I hadn't meant to hurt his feelings, but it was hard to respect a homemade gravestone. "I don't know, Gunnar," I said. "It's like you're getting all Hamlet on me and stuff. I swear, if you start walking around with a skull, and saying 'to-be-or-not-to-be,' I'm outta here."

He looked at me coldly, and said, insulted, "Hamlet was from Denmark, not Sweden."

I shrugged. "What's the difference?"

And to that he said, "Get out of my house."

But since we were in his backyard, and not in his house, I stayed put. He made no move to physically remove me from his presence, so I figured he was bluffing. I looked at that stupid rock that said GUNN in crooked letters. He had already returned to carving. I could hear that his breathing sounded a little bit strained, and wondered whether that was normal, or if the illness was already making it difficult for him to breathe. I had looked up the disease online—Pulmonary Monoxic Systemia had symptoms that could go mostly unnoticed, until the end, when your lips got cyanotic—which means they turn blue, like they do when you're swimming in a pool someone's too stinking cheap to heat. Gunnar's lips weren't blue, but he was pale, and he did get dizzy and light-headed from time to time. Those were symptoms, too. The more I thought I about it, the worse I felt about being so harsh over the tombstone.

Then, on a whim, I reached into my backpack, pulled out a notebook and pen, and began writing something.

"What are you doing?"

"You'll see."

When I was done, I tore the page out of the notebook, held it up, and read it aloud. "'I hereby give one month of my life to Gunnar Ümlaut. Signed, Anthony Bonano.'" I handed it to him. "There. Now you've got borrowed time. Seven months instead of six months—so you don't gotta start digging your own grave for a while."

Gunnar took it from me, looked it over, and said, "This doesn't mean anything."

I expected him to launch into some Shakespearean speech

about the woes of mortality, but instead he showed me the paper, pointing to my signature, and said, "It's not signed by a witness. A legal document must be signed by a witness."

I waited for him to start laughing, but he didn't.

"A witness?"

"Yes. It should also be typed, and then signed in blue ink. My father's a lawyer, so I know about these things."

I still couldn't tell whether or not he was kidding. Usually I can read people—but Gunnar, being Swedish and all, is as hard to figure out as IKEA assembly instructions; even if I think I'm reading him right, it's guaranteed I've done something wrong and I'll have to start over.

Since his expression stayed serious, I thought of something to say that sounded seriously legal. "I'll take it under advisement."

He grinned and slapped me hard on the back. "Excellent. So let's have dinner and watch *The Grapes of Wrath*."

Five places were set for dinner—including one for Mr. Ümlaut, who was presumably working late, but would be home "eventually." Mrs. Ümlaut made hamburgers, although I was expecting something more Scandinavian. I knew about Scandinavian food on account of this Norwegian smorgasbord place my family once accidentally ate at, because it was called DØNNY'S and my parents thought the ø was an *e*. Anyway, there was a lot of food at the buffet, including like fourteen thousand kinds of herring—which I wouldn't touch, but it was satisfying to know there were so many different things I could refuse to eat. I was oddly disappointed that not a single form of herring was on the Ümlauts' menu.

Sitting at the Ümlauts' dinner table that night was not the nerve-racking ordeal I had thought it would be. No one talked about Gunnar's illness, and I didn't say anything too terribly stupid. I talked about the proper placing of silverware, and the cultural reasons for it—something my father made sure to teach me, since I had to put out place settings at the restaurant. It made me look sophisticated, and balanced out anything subhuman I might have done at the table. I even demonstrated my water-pouring skill, pouring from high above the table, and not spilling a drop. It made Kjersten laugh—and I was pretty certain she was laughing *with* me instead of *at* me—although by the time I got home, I wasn't so sure.

Mr. Ümlaut didn't make it in time for dinner. Considering how much my own father worked lately, I didn't think much of it.

Dad came home early from work that night with a massive headache. Nine-thirty—that's early by restaurant standards. He sat at the dining table with a laptop, crunching numbers, all of which were coming up red.

"You could change your preferences in the program," I suggested. "You could make all those negative numbers from the restaurant come up green, or at least blue."

He chuckled at that. "You think we could program my laptop to charm the bank so we don't have to pay our mortgage?"

"You'd need a sexier laptop," I told him.

"Story of my life," he answered.

I thought about talking to him about Gunnar, but his worries tonight outweighed mine. "Don't work too hard," I told him—which is what he always said to me. Of course he usually said it when I was lying on the sofa like a slowly rotting vegetable.

Before I went to bed that night, I took a moment to think about the various weirdnesses that had gone on in Gunnar's backyard that afternoon—particularly the way he acted when I gave him that silly piece of paper. I had written it just to give him a laugh, and maybe get him to shift gears away from dying and stuff. Had he actually taken me seriously?

I opened a blank document on my computer, and typed out a single sentence. Then I pulled up the thesaurus, changed a few key words, found a really official-looking font, put the whole thing in a hairline box, and printed it out:

I, Anthony Paul Bonano, being of sound mind and body, do hereby bequeath one month of my natural life to Gunnar Ümlaut.

_____

Signature

_____

Signature of Witness

I have to confess, I almost didn't sign it. I almost crumpled the thing and tossed it into the trash, because it was giving me the creeps. I'm not a particularly superstitious guy . . . but I do have moments. We all do. Like, when you're walking on the street, and you start thinking about that old step-on-a-crack rhyme. Don't you—at least for a few steps—avoid the cracks? It's not like you really think you're gonna break your mother's back, right? But you avoid the cracks anyway. And when somebody sneezes, and you say "God bless you," you're not saying it to chase away evil spirits—which is why people used to say it in the old days—but you don't feel right if you don't say it.

So here I am, looking at this very legal-looking piece of paper, and wondering what it means to sign away one month of my life. And then I think, if this was an actual contract—if it was true and somewhere in the Great Beyond a tally of days *was* being kept—would I still do it, and give Gunnar an extra month?

Sure I would.

I knew that without even having to think about it.

So I bit back the creepy step-on-a-crack feeling, got a blue pen, and signed my name. Then, during my first class the next morning, I got Ira to sign as witness.

And that's when things began to get weird.

Photo Ops, Flulike Symptoms, and Trident Exchange in the Hallway of Life

4 There are very few things I've done in my life that I would consider truly inspired. Like the time I e-mailed everyone at school to tell Howie his pants were on backward. After dozens of people pulled him aside to tell him, he finally gave in to peer pressure, went into the bathroom, and turned his pants around, so they really *were* on backward.

That was inspired.

Giving Gunnar a month of my life—that was inspired, too. The problem with inspiration, though, is that it's kind of like the flu—once one person gets it, it spreads and spreads until pretty soon everyone's all congested and hawking up big wads of inspiration. It happens whether you want it to or not, and there's no vaccination.

I tracked Gunnar down in the hallway between third and fourth periods that day, and presented him with his extra month, officially signed and witnessed.

He read it over, and looked at me with the kind of gaze you don't want a guy giving you in a public hallway.

"Antsy," Gunnar said, "there are no words to express how this makes me feel."

Which was good, because words might have made me awkwardly emotional, and that would attract Dewey Lopez, the school photographer—who was famous for exposing emotions whenever possible. Such as the time he caught star football jock Woody Wilson bawling his eyes out in the locker room after losing the first game that season. In reality, Woody was crying because had just punched his locker and broken three knuckles, but nobody remembers that part—they just remember the picture—so he got stuck with the nickname "Wailing Woody," which will probably stick to him like a kick-me sign for the rest of his life.

So here we are, Gunnar and me, standing there all ripe for a humiliating Kodak moment, and Gunnar finds the words I had wished he wouldn't: "As Lewis once said to Clark, *'He who would give his life for a friend is more valuable than the Louisiana Purchase, entire.'*" And now all I can think about is what if he hugs me—and what if Dewey gets a picture, and I'm known as "Embraceable Antsy" for all eternity?

But instead Gunnar looks at the paper again and says, "Of course you didn't specify which month you're giving me."

"Huh?"

"Well, each month has a different value, doesn't it? September has thirty days, October has thirty-one, and let's not even mention February!"

I have to admit, I was a little stunned by this, but that's

okay, since stunned is an emotion I can handle. It is, in fact, an acceptable state for me. I was willing to go with Gunnar's practical approach—after all, he was the one who was dying, and I wasn't going to question how he dealt with it. I did some quick counting on my fingers. "You got six months left, right? A seventh month would put you into May. So I'm giving you May."

"Excellent!" Gunnar slaps me on the back. "My birthday's in May!"

That's when Mary Ellen McCaw descends out of nowhere, grabs the paper away from Gunnar, and says, "What's this?"

Just so you know, Mary Ellen McCaw is the under-eighteen gossip queen of Brooklyn. She's constantly sniffing out juicy dirt, and since her nose is roughly the size of Rhode Island, she's better than a bloodhound when it comes to sniffing. I'm sure she knew about Gunnar's illness; in fact, she was probably responsible for broadcasting the information across New York, and maybe parts of New Jersey.

"Give it back!" I demanded, but she just holds the thing out of reach, and reads it. Then she looks at me like I've just arrived from a previously unknown planet.

"You're giving him a month of your life?"

"Yeah. So what?"

"Giving Gunnar a new lease on life? Antsy, that's so sweet!"

This leaves me furtherly stunned, because no one has ever called me sweet—especially not Mary Ellen McCaw, who never had a nice word to say about anybody. I figure at first that maybe she means it as an insult, but the look on her face is sincere.

"What a nice thought!" she says.

I shrug. "It's just a piece of paper."

But who was I kidding? This thing was already much more than a stupid piece of paper. Mary Ellen turns from me to Gunnar, and bats her eyes at him. "Can I donate a month of my life, too?"

I look at her, wondering if she's kidding, but clearly she's not.

Gunnar, all flattered, gives her an aw-shucks look and says, "Sure, if you really want to."

"Good, then it's settled," says Mary Ellen. "Antsy, you write up the contract, okay?"

I don't say anything just yet, as I'm still set on stun.

"Remember to specify the month," says Gunnar.

"And," adds Mary Ellen, "make sure it says that the month comes from the end of my life, not the middle somewhere."

"How could it come from the middle?" I dare to ask.

"I don't know—temporary coma, maybe? The point is, even a symbolic gesture should be clear of loopholes, right?"

Who was I to argue with logic like that?

"So what's it like at the Ümlauts'?"

Howie and Ira were all over me in the lunchroom that day, as if going over to the Ümlauts' was like setting foot in a haunted house.

"Was there medical stuff everywhere?" Howie asked. "My uncle had to build a room addition just for his iron lung—the thing's as big as a car."

"I didn't see anything like that," I told them. "It's not that kind of illness."

"It must have been weird, though," Ira said. I considered telling them about Gunnar's do-it-yourself tombstone, but decided not to turn something so personal into gossip.

"It was fine," I told them. "They're just a normal family. The dad's always off working. Their mom's pretty cool, and Kjersten and Gunnar are just like any other brother and sister."

"Kjersten . . ." Ira said, and he and Howie gave each other a knowing grin. "Did you get some quality time with *her*?"

"Actually, I did. We all had dinner together." Ira and Howie were disappointed at how normal the whole thing was, considering. Still, it didn't stop them from being envious that I actually got to eat a whole meal with Kjersten. I didn't even have to exaggerate. The more I downplayed it, the more jealous they became.

There's something to be said about being the envy of your friends. They made some of the standard rude jokes friends will make about beautiful girls out of their reach—the same ones I was tempted to make myself, but didn't. Then the conversation came back to the subject of death, which is just as compelling and almost as distant as sex.

"Were they all religious and stuff?" Ira asked. "People always get that way when someone gets sick—remember Howie's parents when they thought he had mad cow?"

"Don't remind me," says Howie.

I thought about it, but didn't remember anything like that at the Ümlauts'. They didn't say grace like we do at my house when someone remembers to. Ira was right—if Gunnar was my kid, I'd be saying grace all the time.

"His mom doesn't talk about his illness at all," I told them.

"I guess that's how they deal with it. It's creepy, because there's always, like, an elephant in the room."

Then Howie looks at me with those drowning-penguin eyes, and I know where this is going.

"You're joking right? Is that even legal?"

"Yeah," I tell him, without missing a beat. "It's housebroken, too, and can paint modern art with its trunk."

"Okay," Howie says, getting mad, "now you're just making stuff up."

I could keep this going for hours, but Ira chimes in. "It's an expression, Howie. When something's completely obvious but everyone's ignoring it, you say 'there's an elephant in the room'—because, just like an elephant, it's big and fat, and hard to ignore."

Howie thinks about it and nods. "I get it," he says. "Although that kind of weight gain could be glandular. Is it his mother?"

This time Ira doesn't even throw him a life preserver.

That afternoon I had a second hallway encounter. It was one of those moments that gets burned into your brain like a cigarette on a leather couch. I'm convinced it left me with brain damage.

It was just before last period. I was scrambling to get my math book out of my locker before the tardy bell when I heard a familiar voice behind me saying my name for the third time in as many days.

"Antsy?"

I turned to see none other than Kjersten Ümlaut behind me.

Her eyes were all moist and shiny, and the first thing that struck my brain was that Kjersten was even more beautiful in tears.

"I heard about what you did for Gunnar," she said.

I'm figuring maybe she's gonna slap me for it, so I say, "Yeah, sorry about that. It was a dumb idea."

"I just wanted you to know how thoughtful it was."

"Really?"

"Really. And I wanted to thank you."

And that's when it happened. She kissed me. I think maybe she meant to give me a little peck on the cheek, but I had just closed my locker and was turning, so the kiss landed a bull's-eye on the mouth.

Okay—now you'd think this would be the stuff of dreams and fireworks and time-stopping, *Matrix*-like special effects, right? The thing is, that only happens when you're expecting it and have time to set the moment up. But this was sudden. It was kind of like overcranking a cold car engine. It just grinds instead of starting. And so, what should have been the kiss from heaven was instead the lip-lock from hell.

See, I had just come back from phys ed, where we were running outside in the cold, so my nose was kinda stuffy and I was doing a whole lot of mouth breathing. In other words, my mouth is open like a fish when she comes at me.

The second it happens, a million volts go shooting through my head, and it's too much to handle, so my brain decides to take a Hawaiian vacation—I can almost hear the jet engines as it takes off from LaGuardia—and now the only thing in my head is gratitude that I got my braces off last month, followed immediately by horror, because now she's getting nothing but retainer, and why did I pick today of all days to have salami for lunch, and would the brownie I ate afterward provide enough cover, and where's that mint flavor coming from?

Then in a second I'm hearing bells, and I think it's some sort of mental shell shock, until I realize it's the tardy bell, which means I'll get detention, but none of that matters, because there's Dewey Lopez with his camera, preserving the moment for eternity and saying, "Thanks, guys, that one's a keeper!" and he's gone, maybe to look for my brain on that beach in Maui.

Kjersten finally pulls away, and I say—I swear I actually say this: "Do you want your gum back, or should I keep it?"

She's a little red in the face, or maybe it's green, because I think my brain-burn left me temporarily color-blind.

"Sorry," she says, and I'm thinking it's me who should be saying sorry, but I'm still figuring out what the hell I should do with the gum, and then she says, "Well, I just wanted to thank you. It's just what Gunnar needs."

"Thanks for thanking," I say. "Thank me anytime!" And then she's gone faster than Dewey Lopez.

As for me, I went off to sit in a math class that I have absolutely no memory of.

My experience with girls is limited, and usually ends in pain. The one exception is Lexie Crawley. The crash site of *that* relationship eventually grew flowers, instead of poison ivy and flytraps. In other words, after breaking up, Lexie and I became friends—and it's not like the friendship I've got with Howie and Ira. See, Howie and Ira, they're more like family. You can't get rid of them, so you don't even try, and learn to live with them. It's okay having friends like that, because no matter what direction your life takes, you'll always have the Howies and Iras of the world to raise your self-esteem, because they make you look good by comparison.

But Lexie was different. First of all, she's got insight instead of sight. Being blind doesn't necessarily make a person remarkable, but Lexie has managed to build something wonderful around what others would call a disability. Secondly, Lexie's got more class than anyone I know, and I'm not talking snooty I'm-better-than-you kind of class. I mean real class. I admire her for who she is.

Here's what it's like between Lexie and me: she can tell me that I'm a much better friend than boyfriend, and I can actually take it as a compliment. That's a big deal, because most girls use that "I like you as a friend" line as secret code for "Keep your paws away from me, you slimeball," but not Lexie. I knew if there was anyone I could ask for advice on what Kjersten's kiss really meant, it was her.

I went to Crawley's restaurant straight from school that day, looking for Lexie. Although Crawley also owned most of *Paris, Capisce?*, the original Crawley's is his main restaurant. He and Lexie actually live in it. Sort of. See, it's a huge mansion, but only the first floor is restaurant. The two of them live on the second floor, with fifteen dogs: one for each of the seven deadly sins, and seven virtues, plus one Seeing Eye dog that must have identity issues, because it's the only yellow Lab in a sea of fourteen Afghan hounds.

"What do *you* want?" Old Man Crawley growled when he

answered the door. He always said that to me. Except when he was expecting me. Then he'd say, "You're late!" even if I was early. It wasn't just me he treated this way, though. The whole world was an enemy waiting to happen. According to my father, Crawley's greatest joy came from watching him squirm. In this I could teach my dad a thing or two, because Crawley never made me squirm. I just laughed at him. It annoyed him, but I think he respected me for it.

The dogs barked and pawed me with their usual greeting. Crawley pulled Gluttony back by the collar, and sent him off. Since Gluttony was the alpha male of the pack, the other dogs followed.

"Is it that time already?" Crawley asked as I stepped in.

"You'll never know," I told him with a grin.

"I always know," he said. He was, of course, referring to our monthly kidnapping—the planning of which was usually why I came over to chat with Lexie. Like I said, Crawley had us kidnap him once a month, and force him to do something exhilarating. He even paid me for it. The fact that he's rich and we get to use his money to plan our adventure outings allows us some really unique opportunities. Last month was a dolphin encounter at the Brooklyn Aquarium, with a shark thrown in for added excitement.

"What are you planning for this month?" he asked.

"Space shuttle," I told him. "We're sending you to blow up a comet before it can destroy the earth. You'll be strapped to the tip of the warhead."

"Smart-ass." He poked me with his cane. Although he broke his hip last year, I don't think he needed the cane to walk anymore. I believe he kept it as a weapon.

"So tell me," he asked, "what new things have you botched up at *Paris, Capisce?* lately?"

"You mean besides Thanksgiving? Sorry, but I have no other screwups to entertain you with."

He shook his head and scowled at me, annoyed that I had no humiliating food-service moments to share. "Incredible," he said. "You're disappointing even when you're *not* disappointing." Then he went off into the kitchen, where he was quickly surrounded by amber waves of dog.

Lexie got home ten minutes later and was surprised, but pleased, to find me there. She let Moxie, her Seeing Eye dog, out of his halter, and he came bounding to me, expressing all the emotion that Lexie was too proper to display. She did give me a hug, though.

"I'm glad you came by," she said. "I've been thinking about you."

"You have?" I instantly wondered what she was thinking, and why, and whether I should feel embarrassed, flattered, or awkward.

"There's this new boy at school who sounds like you. I keep hearing him in the lunchroom. It's very distracting."

"Yeah," I said. "If he sounds like me, he must be distracting."

She laughed at that. "It's only distracting because I keep expecting it to be you."

I sat across from her in the living room and got right to business, telling her the reason for my visit. I expected her to be full of wisdom, and maybe give me a road map into the mind of Kjersten Ümlaut. Instead she just folded her arms.

"So let me get this straight," she said. "You're telling me

you've been kissed by a beautiful girl, and you want *me* to give *you* advice about it."

"Yeah, that's the general idea."

I could already tell this was going south. I'm not the most observant guy in the world, but I've learned that reading Lexie's body language is very important. See, lots of people put on fake body language, making you see what they want you to see—but since Lexie doesn't think in terms of sight, her body language is always genuine. And right now she was genuinely peeved.

"So, a girl kissed you. Why does that have to involve me?"

"She's not a girl, she's a JUNIOR, and every guy in school would give their left arm to go out with her—but she kissed *me*."

Still, Lexie's all cross-armed and huffy. Even the dogs are looking at her like there's something wrong.

And then I finally get it.

"Are you jealous?"

"Of course not," she says, but her body language says different.

"How can you be jealous?" I ask. "You're dating that guy who clicks, right?" The guy I'm talking about is this blind dude with the very rare gift of echolocation. By making clicking noises, he can tell you exactly what's around him. It's kind of like human sonar—he's been on the news and everything.

"His name is Raoul," says Lexie, all insulted.

"Yeah, well, if *my* name was Raoul, I'd rather be called 'that guy who clicks.'"

The scowl on her face scares away at least four of the dogs. I figure it's time to backtrack a little bit, so I give her the whole story—about Gunnar, and his weird incurable illness, and the extra month, figuring if she has the background, she might not be so annoyed by the whole thing. The second I mention the free month, she unfolds her arms.

"You gave him a month of your life?"

"Yeah, and that's why his sister kissed me—so she says."

"Antsy, that was a really nice gesture!"

"Yeah, sure, but we're not talking about that right now, we're talking about the kiss."

"Fine, fine—but tell me, what did that boy say when you gave him the month?"

By now I'm getting all exasperated myself. "He said 'thank you,' what do you think he said? Can we get back to the other thing now?"

But if there was any hope of getting advice on the subject, it flew out the window when Old Man Crawley came traipsing in, having eavesdropped on the whole conversation.

"What did he give you in return for signing away a month of your life?" Crawley asked.

I sighed. "Nothing. It was a gift. Kind of a symbolic gesture."

"Symbolism's overrated," said Crawley. "And as a gift, it's just plain stupid. It's not even tax-deductible. You should have gotten something in return."

So out of curiosity I asked, "What do you think a month of someone's life is worth?"

He looked me over, curling his lip like I was a bad piece of fish at the market. "A month of *your* life?" he said. "About a buck ninety-eight," and he left, cackling to himself, profoundly amused at how I had walked right into that one.

"Well," said Lexie, no longer peeved at me. "I think a month of your life is worth a lot more than 'a buck ninety-eight.'" She reached out for my hand, and I moved it right into her path so she didn't have to go searching for it. She clasped it, smiling. Then she sighed and reluctantly said, "As for the kiss, my opinion, as your friend, is that it *does* mean something. There's no such thing as a 'thank-you kiss'. At least not in high school."

People Sign Their Lives Away for
the Dumbest Reasons, but Don't Blame Me,
I Just Wrote the Contract

5 I don't think it's possible not to be selfish. Of course that doesn't mean everyone's gotta be like Old Man Crawley either, but there's a little bit of selfishness in everything. Even when you give something from the bottom of your heart, you're always getting something back, aren't you? It could just be the satisfaction of making someone happy—which makes you feel better about yourself, so you can balance out whatever awful thing you did earlier in the day.

Even Howie, who gets screamed at for always buying the wrong gift for his mother, is getting something out of that; each time he gets smacked for getting flowers his mother is allergic to or something, he's left with the warm-fuzzy feeling of knowing some things never change, and his universe is all solid and stable.

My motivations were getting very muddy when it came to my so-called good deeds for Gunnar, and it was starting to feel more and more like disguised selfishness, because of the Kjersten complication.

Lexie believed that Kjersten's kiss meant something. I put a lot of stock in what she said, not just because I trusted Lexie's judgment, but because deep down, I was pretty sure it meant something, too. At the very least it was an invitation to *make* it mean something. Was it wrong to perpetrate good deeds when attention from Kjersten was one of the perks?

> **I, Mary Ellen McCaw, being of sound mind and body, do hereby bequeath one month of my natural life to Gunnar Ümlaut, that month being the month of June, which shall be taken from the end of my natural life, and not the middle.**
>
> *Mary Ellen McCaw*
> **Signature**
>
> *ANTHONY BONANO*
> **Signature of Witness**

Thanks to Mary Ellen, the word about "time shaving" had spread quickly. She bragged to the known world about how she donated a month of her life to poor, poor Gunnar Ümlaut, and how the idea was all hers, although I may have contributed a piece of paper.

As people were not entirely stupid, they saw right through Mary Ellen and realized she was leeching off of my idea—so the next day about half a dozen people came out of the woodwork wanting to donate some of their time. Gunnar was more than happy to accept whatever months came his way, and Kjersten was sufficiently impressed.

"This is just what Gunnar needs," she said when I showed her Mary Ellen's contract. "I don't know how to thank you."

I could have given her some suggestions.

There was this one girl—Ashley Morales—who was clearly in love with Gunnar—even more so than most of the female student body. She wanted her month to be special. "I want my month to be his last," she told me. "Can you make sure that he knows my month is his last?"

Since no one else had claimed the honor, I was happy to oblige.

> I, Ashley Morales, being of sound mind and body, do hereby bequeath one month of my natural life to Gunnar Ümlaut. The month shall <u>not</u> be this coming May or June, which are months already reserved by others. The month shall be taken from the end of my natural life, and not the middle. The month shall be the absolute <u>last additional month</u> of Gunnar Ümlaut's life, beyond which there shall only be afterlife, if applicable.

Ashley Morales
Signature

Neena Wexler
Signature of Witness

Then there was this other guy who had come from confession, and his priest wanted him to say like fourteen thousand Hail Marys for writing obscene graffiti on the Gowanus Expressway. He negotiated it down to one month of community service. I guess the kid figured a month donated to Gunnar was just as good.

The kid was all worried about it, though, and took it even more seriously than Ashley.

"I don't want to give up a month if I'm gonna croak tomorrow or anything," he told me, "because it means I'll owe days from last month, and I don't need that kind of grief."

"C'mon, it's not like it's real or anything," I remind him. "It's just to make Gunnar feel better."

"Yeah," he says, "but what if turns out to be real after all—like those chain e-mails you gotta forward to ten people, or you die?"

"Those aren't real!" I tell him.

"Yeah," he says. "But how can you be sure . . . ?"

I think about that and get all uncomfortable, because I have been guilty of forwarding those stupid e-mails, too. But I usually just send them to people I don't like.

I sigh. "Okay. What if I make your contract void if you're scheduled to croak before next month? That way you won't owe any days, and you can enter the pearly gates totally free of debt."

He thought about that some more, finally agreed, and happily went back to his priest, mission accomplished.

I, Jasper Horace Januski, being of sound mind and body, do hereby bequeath one month of my natural life to Gunnar Ümlaut, subject to the stuff listed below:

1. The month shall not be this coming May or June, or the last month of Gunnar Ümlaut's life, which are all already reserved by others.

2. The month shall be taken from the end of my natural life and not the middle.

3. The donated month shall be null and void if my own expiration date is less than 31 days from the date of this contract.

Jasper Januski
Signature

Dewey Lopez
Signature of Witness

I have to admit, it felt good to be doing something positive for Gunnar, in spite of the fact that it hadn't brought forth a second kiss from Kjersten, regardless of how little salami I ate, or how much mouthwash I used. I think maybe her reluctance came from the picture Dewey Lopez published in the school paper of our first kiss. Luckily it wasn't on the front cover, since he also snapped a picture of Principal Sinclair coming out of the bathroom with his fly open and a piece of shirttail hanging out. Definitely front-page material. Still, the page-four article was seen by the whole school, with the unpleasant headline LOVE SKIPS A GRADE.

I don't know how it affected Kjersten's social standing, but it sure did elevate mine. Everybody wanted to know about it, but I kept quiet, because I figured Kjersten might respect a guy who didn't kiss and tell—even if that guy was one year and seven months younger than her. (Yes, I snuck into the office and checked her school record to find out exactly how much older than me she was.)

Kjersten never mentioned the article or the picture or, for that matter, the kiss. But she did continue to tell me what an entirely great guy I was, which meant another piece of Trident might only be a few days away.

"It's so, so special that you're sensitive to Gunnar's little problem," Kjersten told me when I handed her the month Howie gave me—which was month number seven and counting.

At the time I had laughed, and wondered how she could call it "a little problem." I'm not wondering anymore. And I'm not laughing either.

I, Howard Bernard Bogerton, being of somewhat sound mind and body, do hereby bequeath one month of my natural life to Gunnar Ümlaut, subject to the stuff listed below:

1. The month shall not be this coming May or June, or the last month of Gunnar Ümlaut's life, which are all already reserved by others.

2. The month shall be taken from the end of my natural life, and not the middle.

3. The donated month shall be null and void if my own

expiration date is less than 31 days from the date of this contract.

4. Should Gunnar Ümlaut use my month for criminal acts such as shoplifting or serial killing, I shall not be held responsible.

HOWIE BOGERTON
Signature

Ira Goldfarb
Signature of Witness

By Friday, I had gotten Gunnar a full year.

A Nasty Herd of Elephants
That Are Nowhere Near as
Embarrassingly Adorable as Me.
Don't Ask.

6 Nobody gets up early on Saturday morning in our house anymore. Friday night's a late night for the restaurant. Mom and Dad are usually up even later than me—and that's saying something. I slunk into the kitchen at around eleven that morning to see Mom, clearly still on her first cup of coffee, trying to comfort an inconsolable Christina.

"But I don't want to put Ichabod to sleep," Christina said through her tears. "It's inhumane."

"It's inhumane to let him suffer." She looked at our cat, who was now lying on the windowsill in the sun. If he was suffering, he wasn't showing it. It was actually the rest of us who were suffering, because poor Ichabod was so old he had forgotten the form and function of a litter box, and had begun to improvise, leaving little icha-bits in unlikely places.

"It's the way of all things, honey," Mom said sympathetically. "You remember Mr. Moby—and what about your hamsters?"

"It's not the same!" Christina yelled.

Mr. Moby was Christina's goldfish. Actually a whole series of goldfish. She named them all Mr. Moby, the same way Sea World named all their star whales "Shamu." Then she graduated to hamsters, which were cute, cuddly, vicious little things that would devour one another with such regularity you'd think cannibalism was in their job description. But Christina was right—this was different. A cat was more like family. Besides, in my current state of mind, mortality was kind of a sore spot.

"Mom," I said, "couldn't we just let nature take its course, and let Ichabod go when he's ready?"

"I'll clean up if he misses the litter box," Christina said. "Promise."

"Yeah," I said. "Maybe she can levitate it out the window."

Christina scowled at me. "Maybe you could give Ichabod one of your friend's extra months."

This surprised me—I didn't even know she knew about that, but I guess word gets around. Fortunately it flew miles over Mom's head.

"You know what?" Mom said. "I'm not gonna worry about this anymore. It's on your head." Then she poured herself a fresh cup of coffee.

I went over to Gunnar's house that afternoon, using our *Grapes of Wrath* project as a cover story, but what I was really hoping for—and dreading at the same time—was seeing Kjersten. It turns out she had left early for a tennis tournament. I was deeply disappointed, and yet profoundly relieved.

We were halfway through *The Grapes of Wrath* and had decided that, for our project, we were going to re-create the dust bowl in Gunnar's backyard, then arrange for our class to come see it. The dust bowl is what they called the Midwest back in the thirties, when Oklahoma, Kansas, and I think maybe Nebraska dried up and blew away—which has nothing to do with *Gone with the Wind*, although that movie was made during the same basic time period.

Mrs. Ümlaut fretted a lot when we told her about our plan. *Fretted:* that's a word they used during the dust bowl. ("Fretted," "reckon," and "y'all" were very popular in those days.) But since the backyard was mostly crabgrass already going dormant for the winter, she reluctantly agreed to let us kill the whole yard as long as we promised to redo everything in the spring. I couldn't help but glance at Gunnar when she said that, because what if he wasn't around in the spring? Then again, maybe this was her way of implying to him that he would be.

I figured the biggest problem with the dust bowl was Gunnar's unfinished gravestone smack in the middle of the yard. By now Gunnar had finished his first name and begun working on his middle name, Kolbjörn, which he was worried wouldn't fit on one line. "I may have to start over on a fresh piece of granite," he told me. I just nodded. I decided it was best if I didn't involve myself in tombstone-related issues.

Before we began murdering helpless vegetation, Gunnar took me up to his room to show me what he had done with the twelve months I had gotten for him. He had three-hole-punched them, and put them in a binder labeled *Life*. He displayed it proudly, like someone else might display a photo album.

"I consulted with Dr. G yesterday," Gunnar said. "He says I might make nine months—maybe more, because my symptoms haven't been getting worse." Then he patted his Binder of Life. "But maybe the real reason's right here."

I let out a nervous chuckle. "Whatever it takes, right?"

I still didn't know if he was serious, or just playing along. The kids who donated their months were, for the most part, treating it like a game. I mean, sure, they were hung up on the rules, but it was more like how you argue over a Monopoly board, and whether or not you're supposed to get five hundred bucks if you land on "Free Parking." The rules say no, but people still insist it's the cash-bonus space. In fact, my cousin Al once busted a guy's nose over it—which sent him directly to jail, do not pass "Go."

The point is, even when a game gets serious, there's still a line between game-serious and *serious*-serious. If I was sure which side of that line Gunnar was on, I'd have felt a whole lot better. Apparently I wasn't the only one who felt a little unsettled around Gunnar. Sure, girls flocked to him, but when it came to our literature circles, they divided right along gender lines, with all the girls going for things that sounded romantic, like *East of Eden*. We had four guys in our group to start with, but they had all migrated to other novels. I suspected their migration was, much like the farmworkers in our book, driven by empty plains of death. In other words, they couldn't handle Gunnar's constant coming attractions about the end of his life.

"I'll never forget," he said to Devin Gilooly, "that you were my first friend when I moved here. Would you like to be a pallbearer?"

Devin went bug-eyed and vampire-pale. "Yeah, sure," he said. The next day, he not only switched to a different novel, he switched to a different English class. If it were possible, I think he would have switched to another school altogether.

"Doesn't your culture ululate for the dead?" Gunnar asked Hakeem Habibi-Jones.

"What's 'ululate'?" Hakeem asked, making it clear that any cultural traditions had been lost in hyphenation. Gunnar demonstrated ululation, which was apparently a high-pitched warbling wail that was maybe meant to wake the dead person in question. All it succeeded in doing was chasing Hakeem away.

After that, it was just Gunnar and me. Even now, as we started pumping out poison in his yard, I was afraid Gunnar would talk about the death of weeds and find a way to relate it to himself, like maybe he was some unwanted plant targeted by the Weedwhacker in the sky.

He didn't talk about himself, though. Instead he talked about me. And his sister.

I was all set to put a painfully ugly shrub out of its misery when Gunnar said, "You know, Kjersten really likes you."

I turned to him, and ended up spraying herbicide on his shoes. "Sorry."

He took it in stride, just wiping the stuff off with a rag. "You shouldn't be surprised," he said. "Not with that kiss all over the school paper."

I shrugged uncomfortably. "It wasn't all over the paper. It was on page four. And anyway, it wasn't really a kiss—it was just a peck. Or at least I think it was supposed to be." But I couldn't help but think about what Lexie had said. "Has Kjersten . . . said anything about it to you?"

"She doesn't have to *say* anything—I know my sister. She doesn't kiss just anybody."

There it was—confirmation from a sibling! "So, are you saying she Likes me, as in 'Like' with a capital *L*?"

Gunnar considered this. "More like italics," he said. Which was fine, because the capital *L* was more than I could handle.

"So . . . are you okay with her *liking* me?"

Gunnar continued to kill the plants. "Why shouldn't I be? Better you than some other creep, right?"

I wasn't sure whether he was REALLY okay with it, or just pretending to be okay with it. The only similar situation in recent memory had to do with Ira's ten-year-old sister, who was kissed in the playground by some twelve-year-old last Valentine's Day. The second Ira heard about it, he assembled a posse to terrorize the kid, and now she might never be kissed again.

This situation was different, though. First of all, *she* kissed *me*, not the other way around. Secondly, she's Gunnar's *older* sister, so it's not like he's got to be protective, right?

"She likes you because you're genuine," Gunnar said. "You're the real thing."

This was news to me. I don't even know what "thing" he meant, so how could I be the real one? But if it's a thing Kjersten liked, that was fine with me. And as for being "genuine," the more I thought about it, the more I realized what a big deal that was. See, there's basically three types of guys at our school: poseurs, droolers, and losers. The poseurs are always pretending to be somebody they're not, until they forget who they actually are and end up being nobody. The droolers have brains that have shriveled to the size of a walnut, which could either be genetic or media-induced. And the losers, well, they eventually find one another in all that muck at the bottom of the gene pool, but trust me, it's not pretty.

Those of us who don't fit into those three categories have a harder time in life, because we gotta figure things out for ourselves—which leaves more opportunity for personal advancement, and mental illness—but hey, no pain, no gain.

So Kjersten liked "genuine" guys. The problem with genuine is that it's not something you can try to be, because the second you try, you're not genuine anymore. Mostly it's about being clueless, I think. Being decent, but clueless about your own decency.

I don't know if I'm genuine, but since I'm fairly clueless most of the time, I figured I was halfway there.

"So . . . what do you think I should do?" I asked, parading my cluelessness like suddenly it's a virtue.

"You should ask her for a date," Gunnar said.

This time I sprayed the herbicide in my eyes.

My advice to you: avoid spraying herbicide in your eyes if at all you can help it. Use a face mask, like the bottle says in bright red, but did I listen? No. The pain temporarily knocked Gunnar's suggestion to the back of my brain, and the world became a faraway place for a while.

I spent half an hour in the bathroom washing out my eyes while Gunnar threw me a few famous quotes about the therapeutic nature of pain. By the time my optical agony faded to a dull throbbing behind my eyelids, I felt like I had just woken up from surgery. Then I step out of the bathroom, and who's coming in the front door? Kjersten.

"Antsy! Hi!" She sounded maybe a little more enthusiastic

than she had intended to. I think that was a good thing. Then she looked at me funny. "Have you been crying?"

"What? Oh! No, it's just the herbicide."

She looked at me even more funny, so I told her, "Gunnar and I were killing plants."

Kjersten apparently had a whole range of looking-at-you-funny expressions. "Is this . . . a hobby of yours?"

I took a deep breath, slowed my brain down—if that's even possible—and tried to explain our whole dust-bowl project in such a way that I didn't sound either moronic or certifiably insane. It must have worked, because the funny expressions stopped.

Then Mrs. Ümlaut called from the kitchen. "Are you staying for dinner, Antsy?"

"Sure he is," Kjersten said with a grin. "He can't drive home with his eyes like that."

"I . . . uh . . . don't drive yet."

She nudged me playfully. "I know that. I was just kidding."

"Oh. Right." The fact that she was old enough to drive and I wasn't was a humiliating fact I had not considered. Until now. As I thought about this, I could tell I was going red in the face, because my ears felt hot. Kjersten looked at me and laughed, then she leaned in close and whispered:

"You're cute when you're embarrassed."

That embarrassed me even more.

"Well," I said, "since I'm mostly embarrassed around you, I must be adorable."

She laughed, and I realized that I had actually been clever. I never knew there could be such a thing as charming humiliation. Gold star for me!

Tonight Mrs. Ümlaut made fried chicken—which was as un-Scandinavian as hamburgers, but at least tonight there was pickled red cabbage, which I suspected had Norse origins but was less offensive than herring fermented in goat's milk, or something like that.

It was just the four of us at first—once more with a plate left for Mr. Ümlaut, like he was the Holy Spirit.

Sitting at the Ümlaut dinner table that night was much more torturous than the first time. See, the first time I was desperately trying not to make an ass of myself, just in case Kjersten might notice. But now that she was certain to notice, it was worse than my third-grade play, where I had to dress in black, climb out of a papier-mâché tooth, and be a singing, dancing cavity. I forgot the words to the song, and since Howie had spent half that morning whistling "It's a Small World" in my ear, that was the only song left in my brain. So when I jumped out of the papier-mâché tooth, rather than standing there in silent stage fright, I started singing all about how it's a world of laughter and a world of tears. Eventually, the piano player just gave up and played the song along with me. When I was done, I got applause from the audience, which just made me feel physically ill, so I leaned over, puked into the piano, and ran offstage. After that, the piano never sounded quite right, and I was never asked to sing in a school play again.

That's kind of how I felt at dinner with the Ümlauts that night—and no matter how attractive Kjersten might have found my embarrassment, it would all be over if the combination of fried chicken, pickled cabbage, and stress made me hurl into the serving bowl.

"I had a consultation with Dr. G today," Gunnar announced just a few minutes into the meal. His mother sighed, and Kjersten looked at me, shaking her head.

"I don't want to hear about Dr. G," Mrs. Ümlaut said.

Gunnar took a bite of his chicken. "How do you know it's not good news?"

"Dr. G *never* gives good news," she said. It surprised me that she didn't want to hear about her son's condition—and that she hadn't even accompanied him to the doctor—but then everybody deals with hardship in different ways.

"I may have more time than originally predicted," Gunnar said. "But only with treatment from experts in the field."

That wasn't quite what he had told me, but I could see there were more layers of communication going on here than infomercials on a satellite dish—which, by the way, I am forbidden to watch since the time I ordered the Ninja-matic food processor. But I suspected that whatever treatments Gunnar was talking about were going to cost more than twelve easy payments of $19.99. Maybe that was it—maybe the cost of medical treatment was the elephant in the room here—although I'm sure that wasn't the only one; the Ümlauts seemed to breed elephants like my sister breeds hamsters.

Then, as if that wasn't enough, an entire new herd arrived. Mr. Ümlaut came home.

I always hear people talk about "dysfunctional families." It annoys me, because it makes you think that somewhere there's this magical family where everyone gets along, and no one ever screams things they don't mean, and there's never a time when sharp objects should be hidden. Well, I'm sorry, but that family doesn't exist. And if you find some neighbors that seem to be the grinning model of "function," trust me—that's the family that will get arrested for smuggling arms in their SUV between soccer games.

The best you can really hope for is a family where everyone's problems, big and small, work together. Kind of like an orchestra where every instrument is out of tune, in exactly the same way, so you don't really notice. But when it came to the Ümlaut orchestra, nothing meshed—and the moment Mr. Ümlaut walked through the front door everything in that house clashed like cymbals.

It started with the dinner conversation. From the moment I heard the key turning in the lock, all conversation stopped. I glanced at Gunnar, who stared into his food. I turned my eyes to Kjersten, who turned her eyes to the clock. And when I looked to Mrs. Ümlaut, she didn't seem to be looking at anything at all.

Mr. Ümlaut came into the kitchen without a word, noticed there was a guest at the table, but didn't comment on it. He took out a glass and dispensed himself some water from the refrigerator door.

"You're home," Mrs. Ümlaut finally said, bizarrely stating the obvious.

He took a gulp of his water, and looked at the table. "Chicken?"

Without standing up, Mrs. Ümlaut reached over and pulled out his chair. He sat down.

I took a moment to size the man up. He was tall, with thin-ning blond hair, small glasses, and a wide jaw that Gunnar was starting to develop. There was a weariness about him that had nothing to do with sleep, and he had a poker face that was com-pletely unreadable, just like Gunnar. To me that was the most uncomfortable thing of all. See, I come from a family where we wear our hearts on our sleeves. If you're feeling something, chances are someone else knows about it even before you do. But this man's heart was somewhere in a safe behind the fam-ily portrait.

"I don't believe we've met," he said to me.

His cool gray eyes made me feel like I was on a game show and didn't know the answer.

"Antsy, this is my dad," Gunnar said.

"Pleased to meet you," I said, then silence fell again as every-one ate.

I don't do well with silence, so I usually take it upon myself to end it. My brother says I'm like the oxygen mask that drops when a plane loses air pressure. "People stop talking and Antsy falls from the ceiling to fill the room with hot air until normal-ity returns."

But what if normality is never going to return, and you know it?

I opened my mouth, and words began to spill out like I was channeling the village idiot. "Working today? Yeah, my dad works on Saturdays, too. We got a restaurant, so he's always working when people are eating, and people are always eat-ing—of course that's different from being a lawyer, though—isn't that what Gunnar said you do? Wow, it must have been hard work becoming a lawyer—a lot of school, just like becoming a doctor, right? Except, of course, you don't gotta practice on dead bodies."

I was feeling light-headed, and then realized I had said all that without breathing. I figured maybe I should have put my own oxygen mask on first before helping others, like you're supposed to.

Gunnar didn't say anything—he just stared at me like you might stare at a car wreck you pass on the side of the road. It was Kjersten who spoke.

"He wasn't at work," she said, almost under her breath.

"More chicken?" Mrs. Ümlaut asked me.

"Yes, please, thank you." But even as I tried to plug my mouth up with food, I couldn't stop myself from talking. "My dad had one of his recipes stolen by a restaurant down the block and he says he should sue—maybe you can be his lawyer, or at least tell him if it makes sense to sue, because I hear it costs more money than it's worth, and then there are like fourteen thousand appeals and no one ever sees a penny—of course I could be wrong, you'd know better than me, right?"

He seemed neither amused nor irritated. I would have felt much more comfortable if he were one or the other. "I'm not that kind of lawyer," he said flatly, between bites of food. Gunnar continued his car-wreck gaze, although I think by now it was a multicar pileup.

"Something to drink, Antsy?" Mrs. Ümlaut asked.

"Yes, please, thank you." She poured me a tall glass of milk, and I quickly began to drink—not because I wanted it, but because I knew that unless I was a ventriloquist and could make words come out of somebody else's mouth, drinking would shut me up for a good twenty seconds, and maybe the urge to blather would go away like hiccups.

It worked. Once the glass was drained, my words were drowned. The rest of the meal was filled with an unnatural silence, in which no one made eye contact with anyone else, least of all with Mr. Ümlaut. I made it through the meal listening to clinking silverware, and the ticking of the clock, until Gunnar finally rapped me on the arm and said, "The dust bowl awaits."

I had never been happier to get away from a dinner table, and it occurred to me that this was the first time in the Ümlaut home that it felt as if someone was dying.

It was dark now, with nothing but the back-porch bulb to light up the backyard. We sprayed until both drums of herbicide were empty. Gunnar had brought with him the silence of the dinner table. It drove me nuts, because, just like with his father, I had no idea what he was feeling or thinking—and although I swore to myself I wouldn't bring it up, I couldn't leave without asking Gunnar the big question.

"So what's the deal with your dad?"

Gunnar laughed at that. "The deal," he said. "That's funny." And that's all he said. He didn't tell me that it was none of my business, he didn't tell me to go take a flying leap. He just brushed it off like the question had never been asked.

He took a quick glance at the instructions on his herbicide canister. "Says here that the plants will all be dead in five days, and then it should be easy to pull them out."

"We could sign over two extra days of life to the plants if

you want to wait until next weekend," I said, and laughed at my own joke.

"That's not funny."

"Sorry."

To be honest, I had no clue what I was and wasn't allowed to laugh at anymore.

The moment was far too uncomfortable, so I tried to salvage it. "Hey, by the way, I think there are still a few people at school willing to donate months, if you still want them."

"Why wouldn't I want them?" he asked. "As Nathaniel Hawthorne said, 'Scrounging for precious moments is the most primary human endeavor.'"

He was always so matter-of-fact about it, you could almost forget what was happening to him. Like the end of his life was just an inconvenience.

"Does it ever . . . scare you?" I dared to ask him.

He took a while before he answered. "A lot of things scare me," he said. Then he looked at his unfinished gravestone in the middle of the dying yard. "No doubt about it—I'm going to have to start over."

Before I left, I stopped by Kjersten's room. She was sitting at her desk, doing homework. I suppose she was the type of student who would do homework on a Saturday. I knocked even though the door was open, because there's this instinct we're born with that says you don't walk into a girl's room uninvited, and even when you're invited, you don't walk in too far unless, of course, you're related to each other, or her parents aren't home.

"Hi," I said. "Whatcha doin'?"

"Chemistry," she said.

"Are you studying whether *we* got chemistry?"

She laughed. I have to say, this whole you're-attractive-when-you're-embarrassed thing was great. It was like a free license to say all the things I'd never actually have the guts to say to a girl, because the more embarrassed it made me to say it, the more it worked in my favor.

She turned her chair slightly toward me as I stepped in. Still riding on the fumes of my chemistry line, I thought I might actually dredge up the guts to sit on the edge of her bed . . . Then I realized if I did, I wouldn't be much for conversation, because the phrase *My God, I'm sitting on Kjersten's bed* would keep repeating over and over in my mind like one of Christina's Himalayan mantras, and I might start to levitate, which would probably freak Kjersten out.

So instead of sitting down, I kind of just stood there, looking around.

"Nice room," I told her. And it was: it said a lot about her. There was a NeuroToxin concert poster on the wall, next to a piece of art that even I could recognize as Van Gogh. There was a mural on her sliding closet doors that she clearly had painted herself. Angels playing tennis. At least I think they were angels. They could have been seagulls—she wasn't that great of an artist.

"I like your mural," I said.

She grinned slightly. "No you don't, but thanks for saying so." Like I said, people can pick up my emotions like a podcast. "I like painting, but it's not what I'm good at," she told me. "That's okay, though, because if I was good, then I'd always worry if I was good *enough*. This way I can enjoy doing it, and I never have to care about being judged."

"In that case," I said, "I really DO like your mural. I wish I had the guts to do things I stink at."

She took a measured look at me. "Like what?" she asked.

Now I was put on the spot, because there were so many things to chose from. I thought of her on the debate team, and finally settled on, "I'm not very good speaking in front of an audience."

"It just takes practice. I could teach you."

"Sure, why not?" I was thrilled by the prospect of her coaching me in verbal expression, even though me being a public speaker was about as likely as angels playing tennis. Or seagulls. "I promise to give speeches even worse than you paint," I told her.

She laughed, I laughed, and then the moment became awkward.

"So . . ." I said.

"So . . ." she said.

What happened next was kind of like jumping off the ten-meter platform at the Olympic pool they built when someone in public planning got high and actually believed the Summer Olympics might come to Brooklyn. A couple of years ago, I stood on that platform for five minutes that seemed like an hour, while my friends watched. In the end the only way I was able to jump was to imagine that I was a nonexistent ultracool version of myself. That way I could trick my self-preservation instinct into believing it wasn't actually me jumping.

Standing there in front of Kjersten, I dug down, found ultracool Antsy sipping on a latte somewhere in my head, and pulled him forth.

"So I was wondering if maybe you'd like go out sometime," I heard myself say. "A movie, or dinner, or trip to Paris, that kinda thing."

"Paris sounds nice," Kjersten said. "Will we fly first class?"

"No way!" I told her. "It's by private jet, or nothing." I was dazzling myself with my own unexpected wit, but then ultra-cool Antsy left for Starbucks, and I was alone to deal with the fallout of his cleverness.

"A movie would be nice," she said.

"Great . . . uh . . . yeah . . . uh . . . right." This is like the guy who lifts a five-hundred-pound barbell, then realizes he has no idea how to put it down without dying in the process. "A movie's a good choice," I told her. "It's dark, so people you know won't see us together."

"Why would that matter?"

"Well, you know—you being older and all."

"Antsy," she said, in a lecturing tone that really made her sound older, "that doesn't matter to me."

"Well, good," I said, enjoying the prospect of walking into the multiplex with Kjersten. "And anyway, a movie-theater date will give me lots of great opportunities to be embarrassed."

"I certainly hope so," she said, smirking. Which of course made me go red, which of course made her smirk even more.

This was all going so well! It would have been perfect, except for the fact that her father was weird, and her brother was dying. She must have read what I was thinking, because her smile faded and she looked away.

"I'm sorry about my father," she said.

I shrugged, playing dumb. "He didn't do anything."

"He came home," she said. "These days, that's enough."

Even though I was curious, I didn't want to ask what she meant, just in case she didn't want to tell. I looked at the mural, giving her time to gather her thoughts. Then she said, "He was a partner in a law firm, but a few months ago the firm fell apart. He hasn't worked since."

"But he's gone all the time—what does he do all day, look for work?"

And Kjersten said, "We don't know."

Recipes for Disaster from
the Undisputed Master of Time,
Live on Your TV Screen

7 After my Kjersten encounter, I walked home, nearly getting run over twice on the way, because my head was stuck in an alternate universe. Everything Ümlaut was one step removed from reality; the way they dealt with Gunnar's illness; the Mystery of the Disappearing Dad—even the fact that Kjersten was going to date me was weird, although it was the kind of weirdness I needed more of in my life.

My own father's arrival at home later that same night didn't raise the homeland security index, as it did in the Ümlaut household. That was mainly because everyone but me was already in bed.

"Hi, Antsy," he said as he shuffled into the kitchen. "You're up late."

"Just came down for a drink," I told him, even though I'd been stalking around the house all night with thoughts of Kjersten and Gunnar clogging up my brain. We sat down at the table. He grabbed himself some leftovers from the fridge, and I ate a little, even though I wasn't hungry. I thought it was strange how he can be at a restaurant all night, then come home and have to eat leftovers.

"I heard your friend is real sick," he said. "I'm sorry."

That surprised me. "I didn't know you knew about it."

"Your sister keeps me informed on things."

I could tell he wanted to say something meaningful. Thoughtful. But whenever he opened his mouth, all that came out was a yawn, which made me yawn, and pretty soon whatever he wanted to say got KO'd by the sandman. We left the dirty dishes in the sink, too tired to put them in the dishwasher, and said our good nights.

It was like this more and more between us—more yawning, and less talking. For my father, the restaurant was like the crabgrass in Gunnar's backyard. It had taken over everything. Even on Monday, which was supposed to be his day off, he would do taxes, or go to the fish market to get a jump on the fancy Manhattan restaurants. I think I liked it better when he had a mindless corporate job. His work was miserable, but when he wasn't working, he did stuff. Now, instead of a job and a paycheck, he had a business and a "calling"—as if feeding Brooklyn was a holy mission.

As I went to bed that night, I thought about Mr. Ümlaut, and the weirdness that filled that house like a gas leak. If nothing else, I could be thankful that my own family weirdness was not lethal.

I got a call from Lexie on the way to school the next morning.

"I want to make sure you're free on Saturday the nineteenth," she said.

"Let me check with my social secretary." I glanced over at some fat guy sitting next to me on the bus. "Yeah, I'm free." And then I realized with a little private glee that I might actually need to keep a social calendar now, if things worked out with Kjersten.

The nineteenth was the first day of Christmas vacation, when rich people went off to exotic places where they hate Americans. Sure enough, Lexie said, "My parents are flying me to the Seychelles, to spend the holidays with them," and she added "again," as if it would make me feel better to know she was legitimately embarrassed by her lap of luxury. "They haven't bothered to visit since the summer, so I have to go—but before I do, I've planned a special adventure for Grandpa."

The phone signal kept going in and out—all I heard was something about a team of engineers and lots of steel cable.

"Sounds like fun," I told her. Sure, I could do it. It's not like "vacation" was in my family's vocabulary since the restaurant opened. Then she got to the real reason for her call.

"Oh, and by the way, I'm having dinner at the restaurant with Raoul, and you're invited."

By "the restaurant," I knew she meant Crawley's, her grandfather's first restaurant. By "you're invited," she could have meant a whole lot of things.

"Just me?" I asked.

"No. You . . . and a date . . . if you like."

Now I knew what "you're invited" actually meant. "Wow—an invitation to a five-star restaurant for me and a date. Wouldn't it be easier to put one of those electronic tags on my ear before you release me into the wild?"

She huffed into the phone.

"Admit it—you just want to keep track of me."

She didn't deny it, she just continued the hard sell. "Don't you think whatserface will be impressed if you take her out for a fancy lobster dinner on your first date?"

"How do you know it's our first date?"

"Is it?"

"Maybe it is, maybe it isn't."

She huffed again. I was really enjoying this.

"C'mon," she said, "are you going to turn down a free meal at one of Brooklyn's most expensive restaurants?"

"Ooh! Manipulating me with money," I teased. "You're sounding more and more like your grandfather every day."

"Oh, shut up!"

"Admit it—you're curious to know what kind of girl would kiss me in a school hallway."

At last she caved. "Well, do you blame me? And besides, I really want you to meet Raoul. It's important to me."

"Why? It's not like you need my approval to be dating him."

"Well," she said after a moment's thought, "I'll give you mine, if you give me yours."

Lexie was right about me not being able to turn down the invitation. She had pushed my buttons, and we both knew it. It wasn't the money thing—it was the fact that I desperately wanted to impress Kjersten.

I arrived at school in full grapple with the concept of going on a date with an ex-girlfriend, a prospective girlfriend, and a guy who clicks. I was so distracted, I had to go back to my locker twice for things I forgot, making me late for my first period. Even before I sat in my seat, the teacher handed me a yellow slip summoning me to the principal's office for crimes unknown. People saw the yellow slip and reflexively leaned away.

This was my first experience in a high school principal's office. I don't know what I was expecting that would be different from middle school. Fancier chairs? A minibar? I wasn't scared, like I used to be when I was younger—I was more annoyed by the inconvenience of whatever punishment was forthcoming.

Our principal, Mr. Sinclair, tried to be an intimidating administrator, but he just couldn't sell it. It was his hair that undermined him every step of the way. Everyone called it "The Magic Comb-over." Because if you were looking at him straight-on—the way he might see himself in a mirror—he actually appeared to have hair. But when viewed from any other angle, it became clear that he had only twelve extremely long strands woven strategically back and forth over a scalp that had suffered its own human dust bowl.

It was even harder to take him seriously today, because as I stepped into his office I could see his tie was flipped over his shoulder. There's only one reason a guy has his tie flipped over his shoulder. If you haven't figured it out, you don't deserve to be told.

So I'm sitting there, trying to decide which is worse: pointing out that his tie is over his shoulder and embarrassing him, or not saying anything, which would make it even more embarrassing once he realized it for himself. Either way he'd take it out on me, so this was a lose-lose situation. What made it worse is that I couldn't stop smirking about it.

He poured himself a glass of sparkling water, offering me some, but I just shook my head.

"Mr. Bonano," he said in his serious administrative voice, "do you know why I've called you in?"

I couldn't take my eyes off his tie. I snickered and tried to disguise it as a cough. I sensed myself about to launch into a full-on giggle fit, and I prayed for a light fixture to fall from the ceiling and knock me unconscious before I could—because then I'd become sympathetic.

"I said, do you know why I called you in?"

I nodded.

"Good. Now let's talk about this situation with Gunnar Ümlaut."

"Your tie's over your shoulder," I said.

There was a brief moment where I could tell he was thinking, *Should I just leave it there, and insist it's there for a reason?* But in the end, he sighed, and flipped the tie down . . . right into the glass of sparkling water.

By now, my eyes are tearing from holding back the laughter—and then he says, "I never liked this tie anyway," so he takes it off, and drops it in the trash.

That's when I lost it. Not a giggle fit. No—this was an all-out raging guffaw fest; the kind that leaves your insides hurting and your limbs quivering when you're done.

"HahahahahahahahaI'msorry," I squealed. "Hahahahahahaha can'thelpithahahahahaha."

"I'll wait," said the man who had the power to expel me.

I tried to stop by tensing all my muscles, but that didn't work. Finally I made myself imagine the look on my mother's face when she found out I was expelled from the New York City Public School System for laughing at my principal, and that image drowned my laughter just as effectively as the sparkling water had drowned his tie.

"Are you done?"

I took a deep breath. "Yes, I think so."

He waited until the last of my convulsions faded, pouring the glass of sparkling water into a bonsai at the edge of his desk. "What's life if we can't laugh at ourselves?" he said. Oddly, I found myself respecting him all of a sudden, for the way he kept his cool.

"How many hours?" I asked, not wanting to draw this out any longer than necessary.

"I'm not sure I understand the question?"

"I got detention, right? Because of the stuff with Gunnar. I just want to know how many hours? Does it include Saturday school? Do my parents have to know, or can we keep this between you and me?"

"I don't think you understand, Anthony." And then he smiled. It's not a good thing when principals smile.

"So . . . I'm suspended? C'mon, it's not like I hurt anybody— it's only pieces of paper—I was trying to make the guy feel better about dying and all. How many days?"

"You're not in trouble," said Principal Sinclair. "I called you in because I wanted to donate a month of my own."

I just stared at him. Now it was his turn to laugh at me, but he didn't bust up laughing like I did, he just chuckled. "Actually," he said, "I'm impressed by what you've started. It shows a level of compassion I rarely see around here."

"So . . . you want me to write you up a contract?"

"For me, and for the secretaries in the front office—and for Mr. Bale."

"The security guard wants to give a month, too?"

"You've started a schoolwide phenomenon, Anthony. That poor boy is lucky to have a friend like you."

He gave me a list of names to write contracts up for, and I was a little too shell-shocked to say much more. Then, just before I left, I looked into the trash can. "Keep that tie," I told him. "Throw away the yellow paisley one. *That's* the one everyone makes fun of."

He looked at me like I had just given him an early Christmas gift. "Thank you, Anthony! Thank you for letting me know."

I left with a list of five names, and the strange, unearthly feeling that comes from knowing your principal doesn't hate your guts.

Following up on his schoolwide-phenomenon speech to me, Principal Sinclair insisted that I go on Morning Announcements, to make the whole donated-month thing legitimate school business.

Morning Announcements are kind of a joke at our school. I mean, we got all this video equipment, right, but no one knows how to use it. There's an anchor girl who reads cue cards like she's still stuck in the second level of Hooked on Phonics. And let's not forget the kid who has the nervous habit of adjusting himself on-air whenever he's nervous—which is whenever he's on-air. Occasionally Ira would submit a funny video, but lately there hasn't been much worth watching.

"Just read your lines off the cue cards," the video techie told me, but like I said, public speaking ranks right up there with being eaten alive by ants on my list of unpleasant activities.

After doing my own morning announcement, I now know firsthand why those other kids look like idiots on TV, and I have new respect for Crotch Boy and Phonics Girl.

"Hello, I'm Anthony Bonano with news for you. As many of you know, our friend Gunnar Ümlaut has been diagnosed with PMS, which is a rare life-threatening disease, pause, so I'm asking you, point at camera, to open up your hearts and donate a month of your life as a symbolic gesture, to show Gunnar that we really care. And in return, you'll get a T-shirt that says 'Gunnar's Time Warriors.' Really? There's a T-shirt? Cool! Our goal is to collect as much time as possible. Remember, 'Don't be a dunth. Donate a month.' Now excuse me while I go beat the crap out of whoever wrote that. Did I just say crap on live TV?"

Crotch Boy, Phonics Girl, and now the Blithering Wonder.

It began even before I went to my next class. I was grabbed in the hallway by people who didn't seem to care how moronic I looked on TV. They all wanted to make time donations. Everyone had their own reason for it. One guy did it to impress his girlfriend. One girl hoped it would get her into the popular crowd. Although I didn't want to spend all my free time at my computer printing out time contracts, I couldn't just walk away from what I had started, could I? Besides—there was a kind of power to being the go-to guy. The Master of Time. I even felt like I should start dressing for the part, you know? Like wearing a shirt and tie, the way the basketball team does on the day of a big game. So I found this tie covered with weird melting clocks designed by some dead artist named Dolly. Okay, I admit it, this was really starting to go to my head—like when Wendell Tiggor said he wanted to donate some time.

"You can't," I told him, "on account of Gunnar needs *life,* not wastes-of-life."

The thing is, Tiggor's famous for having really lame comeback lines, like, "Oh yeah? If I'm a waste of life, then you're a stupid stupidhead." (Sometimes the person he was insulting would have to feed him a decent comeback line out of pity.)

This time, however, Tiggor didn't even try. He just pouted and slumped away. Why? Because the Master of Time had spoken, and he was deemed unworthy.

What happened next, well, I guess I could blame it on Skaterdud, but it's not his fault—not really. I blame it on Restless Recipe syndrome. That's something my father once taught me.

It was a month or so before the restaurant first opened, and he was trying to figure out what the official menu would be. It was the first time in his life he'd been forced to write down recipes he had always just kept in his head.

He and Mom were in the kitchen together, cooking one meal after another, which we were giving away to neighbors, because not even Frankie could eat an entire menu. Mom had taken courses in French cooking last year, after finally admitting that Dad was the better Italian chef. It was her way of staking out new taste-bud territory. They had created these fusion French-Italian dishes, but that particular night as they cooked, Dad kept having to stop Mom from adding new ingredients.

"You know what your mother's problem is?" he said to me as they cooked. He knew better than to ever criticize Mom directly. It always had to be bounced off a third person, the way live TV from China has to bounce off a satellite. "She suffers from 'Restless Recipe syndrome.'"

Mom's response was to throw me a sarcastic "Oh, please" gaze, that I would theoretically relay back to my father at our stove somewhere in Beijing.

"It's true! No matter what recipe she's cooking, she can't leave it alone—she has to change it."

"Listen to him! As if he doesn't do the exact same thing!"

"Yes—but at a certain point I stop. I let the recipe be. But your mother will get a recipe absolutely perfect—and then the next time she cooks it, she's gotta add something new. Like the time she put whiskey in the marinara sauce."

It made me laugh when he mentioned it. Mom had added so much whiskey, we all got drunk. It's a cherished family memory that I'll one day share with my children, and/or therapist.

Finally she turned to talk to him directly. "So—I didn't cook out the alcohol enough—big deal. I'll have you know I saw that on the Food Channel."

"So go marry the Food Channel."

"Maybe I will."

They looked at each other, pretending to be annoyed, then Dad reached around and squeezed her left butt cheek, she grinned and grabbed his, then the whole thing became so full of inappropriate parental affection, I had to leave the room.

I'm like my father in lots of ways, I guess, but in this respect I'm like my mother. Even when the recipe's working perfectly, I can never leave well enough alone.

With about a dozen time contracts to fill out—each one a little bit different—I tried to hurry home from school that day, hoping to avoid anyone else who wanted to shave some time off their miserable existence. That's when I ran into Skaterdud. At first he rolled past me on his board like it was just coincidence, but a second later he looped back around. He flustered me with his eight-part handshake before he started talking.

"Cultural Geography, man," he said, shaking his head—it was a class we were both in together. "I just don't get it. I mean—is it culture? Is it geography? You know where I'm going, right?"

"The skate park?" I answered. Sure, it was closed for the winter, but that never stopped Skaterdud before.

"I'm talking conceptually," he said. "Gotta follow close or you're not never gettin' nowhere."

I've learned that silence is the best response when you have no idea what someone is talking about. Silence, and a knowing nod.

"I'm thinking maybe one favor begets another, *comprende*?"

I nodded again, hoping he hadn't suddenly become bilingual. It was hard enough to understand him in one language.

"So you'll do it?" he asked.

"Do what?" I had to finally ask.

He looked at me like I was an imbecile. "Write my Cultural Geography paper for me."

"Why would I do that?"

"Because," he said, "I'm gonna give up six whole months of my life to your boy Gunnar."

That got my interest. No one had offered that much. The Master of Time was intrigued.

Skaterdud laughed at the expression on my face. "Ain't no biggie," he said. "It's not like it's never gonna matter—'cause don't I already know when I'm gonna be pushin' up posies? Or seaweed, in my case? *That* date with destiny ain't never gonna change, because the fortune-teller's prediction would have already taken into account whatever life I'd give away to Gunnar. Smart, right? Yeah, I got this wired!"

I was actually following his logic, and it scared me. "So . . . why just six months?" I said, playing along. "If your future's all set in stone no matter what you do, why not give a year?"

"Done," said Skaterdud, slapping me on the back. "Don't forget—that Cultural Geography paper's due Friday."

"Whoa! Wait a second! I didn't say it was a deal." I was getting all mad now, because I felt like I was a sucker at a carnival, and had gotten tricked into this—so I said the first thing that came to mind, which, sadly, was: "What's in it for me?"

Skaterdud shrugged. "What do you want?"

I thought about how stockbrokers get commissions when they make a deal, so I thought, *Why not me?* "One extra month commission for me. Yeah, that's it. An extra month to do with as I please."

"Done," he said again. "Let me read the paper before you turn it in so I know what I wrote."

I, Reginald Michaelangelo Smoot, aka Skaterdud, in addition to the twelve months donated to Gunnar Ümlaut in the attached contract, do hereby bequeath one month to Anthony Paul Bonano for his own personal use in any way he sees fit, including, but not limited to:

    A.) Extending his own natural life.

    B.) Extending the life of a family member or beloved pet.

    C.) Anything else, really.

R.M. Smoot

Signature

Ralphy Sherman

Signature of Witness

Who Needs Cash When You've Got Time Coming Out of Your Ears?

8 I have never been in the habit of cheating at school. I mean, sure, the occasional glance at my neighbor's paper on a multiple-choice test or a list of dates written on my forearm, but nothing like what Skaterdud wanted me to do. Now not only did I have to write two passing papers, but I had to make one of them sound like he wrote it—which meant sounding all confusing but making enough sense to get a passing grade.

The Dud's paper got a B with an exclamation point from the teacher, and since I used all the good stuff in his paper, I got a C-minus on mine. Serves me right. The Dud gave me my month commission the morning we got our grades back, slapped me on the back when he saw my grade, and said, "You'll do better next time."

That day I went off campus to get pizza for lunch, because the lunch ladies were secretly spreading the word that this was a good day to do a religious fast.

Problem was, I didn't have any money. Rishi, who ran the

pizza place down the street, was Indian. Not Native American, but Indian Indian—like from India—and, as such, made pizza that was nothing like the Founding Fathers ever envisioned. Not that it was bad—actually each type he made was amazing, which is maybe why the place was always crowded, and he could keep raising his prices.

I stood there, drooling over a Tandoori Chicken and Pepperoni that had just come out of the oven, and began rummaging through my backpack for spare change—but all I came up with were two nickels, and a Chuck E. Cheese game token that came out as change from one of those high-tech vending machines that was either defective or knew exactly what it was doing.

Rishi looked at me, and just shook his head. Meanwhile the people in line behind me were getting impatient. "C'mon," said Wailing Woody, his beefy arm around his girlfriend's shoulder. "Either order or get out of the way."

What I did next was probably the result of low blood sugar. I opened my binder to see if maybe some coins got stuck under the clasp, and saw the page I had gotten from Skaterdud. My commission. I pulled it out, looked once more at the pizza, and desperately held it up to Rishi.

"I don't have cash, but what about this?" I said. "One month of some guy's life."

A couple of people in line snorted, but not everyone. After all, I had been on Morning Announcements. I was legit. People actually got quieter, waiting to see what Rishi would do. He took it from me, laughed once, laughed twice, and I figured my religious fast was about to begin . . . until he said, "What kind of pizza would you like?"

I was still staring at him, waiting for the punch line, when Woody nudged me and said, "Order already!"

"Uh . . . how many slices is it worth?"

"Two," Rishi said, without hesitation, like it was written on the menu.

I ordered my two slices of Tandoori Chicken-and-Pepperoni, and as he served them he said to me, "I shall frame this and hang it on the wall, there." He pointed to a wall that held a bunch of photos of minor celebrities like the Channel Five weatherman, and Cher. "It will be the cause of much conversation! Next!"

At this point, I'm just figuring I'm lucky—that this is a freak thing. But like I said, other people saw this—people who hadn't eaten, and maybe their brains were working like that high-tech vending machine, which, when I got back to school, gave me a can of Coke for a Chuck E. Cheese token, thinking it was a Sacagawea dollar coin.

The second I popped that soda open, Howie appeared out of nowhere, in a very Schwa-like way, complaining of the kind of thirst that ended empires. "Please, Antsy, just one sip. I swear on my mother's life I won't backwash."

I took a long, slow guzzle from the can, considering it. Then I said, "What's it worth to you?"

I walked away with two weeks of his life.

There's this thing called "supply and demand." You can learn about this in economics class, or in certain computer games that simulate civilizations. You also can blow up those civilizations with nuclear weapons—which is only fun the first couple of times, and then it's like enough already—why spend three hours building a civilization if you're just gonna blow it up? That's three hours of your life you're never gonna get back—and ever since time shaving became a part of my daily activities, I've become very aware of wasted time—whether it be time wasted on the couch watching reruns, or time spent destroying simulated nations. When I first got that game, by the way, it cost fifty bucks, but now you can get it in the sale bin for $9.99. *That's* supply and demand. When everybody wants something and there's not enough to go around, it costs more. But if nobody wants it, it costs next to nothing. In the end, it's people who really decide how much something is worth.

As the undisputed Master of Time, I was the one in complete control of the time-shaving industry. That meant I controlled the supply, and now that I knew I could trade time for other stuff, I began to wonder how big the demand could be.

Turns out I didn't have to wait long to find out. The next morning, Wailing Woody Wilson came to me with his girlfriend to settle a dispute.

"I forgot we had a date last night, and Tanya was all mad at me."

"I'm still mad at you," Tanya reminded him. She crossed her arms impatiently and chewed gum in my general direction.

"Yeah," said Woody. "So I said I'd give her a month of my life." Then he looked at me pleadingly, like I had the power to make it all better.

Well, maybe I'm psychic, or maybe I'm smart, or maybe my stupidity quotient was equal to theirs, because I had anticipated just this sort of thing. In fact, the night before, I had printed out a dozen blank contracts—all they needed to do was fill in the names. I reached into my backpack and pulled a contract out of my binder . . . along with a certificate that would give me my own bonus week as payment for the transaction.

"Oh, and while we're at it," said Woody, "I'll throw in a month for Gunnar, too."

Tanya stenciled hearts all over her certificate, had it laminated, and posted it on the student bulletin board for the whole world to see. From that moment on, any guy who was not willing to give a month of his life to his girlfriend didn't have a girlfriend for long. I was swamped with requests. And on top of romantic commerce, there were other kids who came to me with same-as-cash transactions.

"My brother says he'll give me the bigger bedroom for a month of my life."

"I broke a neighbor's window, and I can't afford to pay for it."

"Could this be used as a Bar Mitzvah gift?"

Between all this new business, and the months that were still pouring in for Gunnar, I was collecting commissions left and right. In a few days I had thirty weeks of my own—which I was able to trade for everything from a bag of chips to a ride home on the back of a senior's motorcycle. I even got a used iPod; trading value: three weeks.

I could not deny the fact that I was getting amazing mileage out of Gunnar's imminent death. I felt guilty about it, since I never got permission from Gunnar to shamelessly use his terminality but as it turns out, Gunnar was actually pleased about it. "*Misery loves company, but it loves power to a greater degree,*'" he said, quoting Ayn Rand. "If my misery has the power to change your life, I'm happy."

Which I guess was okay—if he could be happily miserable, it was better than being miserably miserable—and Gunnar was definitely the most "up" down person I knew.

Even so, I couldn't tell him about the daydreams. Some things are best kept to oneself. See, you can't help the things you daydream about—and they're not always nice. In fact, sometimes they're more nightmares than dreams. Daymares, I'd guess you'd call them. Like the times you get all caught up imagining irritating arguments you never had but might have someday—or the daymares where you put yourself through worst-case scenarios. The sinkhole daymare, for example. See, a while back there was this news report about a sinkhole that opened up beneath a house in Bolivia or Bulgaria, or something. One morning in this quiet neighborhood, there's all this moaning and groaning in the walls, and then the ground opens up, a house plunges a hundred feet into the earth, and everyone inside is swept away in an underground river that nobody knew about except for some braniac in a nearby university who's been writing papers about it for thirty years, but does anybody read them? No.

So you get a daymare about this sinkhole, and what if it happened right beneath your house. Imagine that. You wake up one morning, hit the shower, and as you're drying off, suddenly the ground swallows your entire house, and there you are wrapped in a towel, trying to figure out which is more important at the moment—keeping the towel on, or keeping from being washed away in the underground river?

In these daymares you always survive—although occasionally you're the only one, and it ends with you telling the news reporters how you tried so desperately to save your family, if only they could have held on and been strong like you.

My current recurring daymare involved me at Gunnar's funeral. I'm there and it's raining, because it's always raining at funerals, and all the umbrellas are always black. Why is that? What happens to all those bright flowery umbrellas, or the Winnie-the-Pooh ones? So anyway, there I am holding a depressingly black umbrella with one hand, and my other hand is holding Kjersten, comforting her in her grief. I'm strong for her, and that makes us even closer—and yeah, I'm all broken up, but I don't show it except for maybe a single tear down one cheek. Then someone asks me to say something. I step forward, and unlike in real life, I say the perfect thing that makes everyone smile and nod in spite of their tears, and makes Kjersten respect me even more. And then I snap myself out of it, seriously disgusted that in my head, Gunnar's funeral is all about me.

In a couple of days I had gone through my entire paper supply printing out time-contract forms, and donations were still pouring in. The student council, refusing to be outdone by a lowly commoner like me, put up a big cardboard thermometer outside the main office. I was instructed to notify them daily how much time had been collected for Gunnar so they could mark it off on the thermometer. The goal they set was fifty years, because fifty additional years would make Gunnar sixty-five, and they felt that giving him time beyond retirement age would just be silly.

"It's amazing how generous people can be when you're dying," Gunnar said when I handed him the next stack of months.

"So what's the word from Doctor G?" I asked him. "Any good news?"

"Dr. G is noncommittal," Gunnar told me. "He says I'll be fine, until I'm not."

"That's helpful." I wondered which was worse, having a disease with few symptoms, or one with enough symptoms to let you know where you stood. "Well," I offered lamely, "at least your lips haven't gone blue."

Gunnar shrugged, and swayed a little, like maybe he was having one of his dizzy spells.

"So . . . you think you might make it all the way through next year?" I asked.

Gunnar looked at the stack of time in his hands. "It's possible that I could linger."

Which was more than I could say for his backyard. I went over to his house that Wednesday to continue work on the dust bowl. It was hard spending time in the Universe of Ümlaut now. There were just too many things hanging in the air. Gunnar's imminent death, for example. And the weirdness with their father, and then there was the looming date with Kjersten.

I know that a date with the girl of your dreams shouldn't "loom," but it does. It's worse when you gotta see each other *after* you've asked her out but *before* the actual date. It's kind of like saying good-bye to somebody and then realizing you both gotta get in the same elevator. You can't talk because you already said good-bye, so usually you both stand there feeling like idiots.

So now I'd asked Kjersten out, she said yes, and here I was at her house two days before the actual date. I knew as soon as she got home from tennis practice, it would be elevator time.

As for the Ümlaut backyard, it was officially dead—nothing had survived our herbicidal assault. Even a few of the neighbors' plants had suffered, because the herbicide had seeped into their soil a bit.

"That's what you call 'collateral damage,'" Gunnar said. He looked at the growing desolation around us. "Maybe we can hire some bums and urchins to populate the scene."

Right about then Mrs. Ümlaut called from the house, asking if we wanted hot chocolate since it was getting cold. Instead we asked for "a cuppa joe straight from the pot," which was satisfyingly Steinbeck-like. Of course it would have worked better if she hadn't brought out an automatic-drip glass pot with a floral design.

That's when Kjersten got home, and came out to say hello. I was happy to see her, in spite of it feeling awkward.

"I hear you're the school's official Cupid," she said with a smirk, obviously referring to the new currency of love in our school, for which I was supplying the paperwork.

"I don't shoot the arrows, I just load the bow."

Gunnar groaned and rolled his eyes at that. The smile Kjersten had for me faded when she looked at the big hunk of granite in the middle of our dust bowl. I had gotten so used to seeing the unfinished tombstone there, I had forgotten about it.

"You should move that thing," Kjersten told him. "It's an eyesore."

"Naa," Gunnar said. "People died in the dust bowl, so having a gravestone makes it more authentic."

Kjersten threw me a look, but I turned away. I knew better than to put myself in the middle of this. Instead I just busied myself brushing dirt clods off my jeans.

"Are you staying for dinner?" Kjersten asked.

"No," I told her, way too quickly. "I'm working at my dad's restaurant tonight." After the last Ümlaut meal, I'd rather be pushing menus and pouring water than having to sit at that table again. I think I'd rather be ON the menu than have to eat with their father, if he came home.

Kjersten must have read my mind, because she said, "It's not always that bad."

"Yes it is," said Gunnar, chugging some of the hot coffee.

"Do you always have to be so negative?" Kjersten asked. I wanted to tell her that maybe she should cut her dying brother a little slack, but siding against a prospective girlfriend in any situation is unwise.

Gunnar shrugged. "I'm not being negative, I'm just telling the truth." Then he glanced at the coffeepot. "Just like Benjamin Franklin said, *'Truth can only be served from a scalding kettle; whether you blister or make tea is up to you.'*"

Kjersten gave him a disgusted look that actually made her appear slightly less beautiful, which I hadn't thought was possible. "My brother's nowhere near as smart as he thinks he is."

Then she turned to storm off.

"I'm smart enough to know where Dad goes," said Gunnar.

It stopped Kjersten in midstorm, but only for an instant. Then she picked up her stride and continued inside, without even turning back to give Gunnar an ounce of satisfaction.

Once she was gone, Gunnar and I continued to hurl plants into Hefty bags in silence. Now that Kjersten had reminded me of the gravestone, I couldn't stop looking at it. The elephant in the dust bowl. But for once Gunnar wasn't obsessing over his own eventual doom. His thoughts were somewhere else entirely.

"Three times," Gunnar said, finally breaking the silence. "Three times I checked the odometer in my dad's car before he left and after he got back, then did the math. All three times, he traveled somewhere that was between a hundred and thirty and a hundred and forty miles away."

It was good detective work, I guess, but was only half the job. "It doesn't mean much if you don't know which direction he's going."

"Try northwest." Then Gunnar reached into his pocket and flipped me a red disk. "I found this in his car." Even before I caught it, I knew what it was.

"A poker chip? He's playing poker?"

"Probably blackjack or craps," Gunnar said "Take a closer look."

The chip was red with black stripes around the edge. There was an *A* printed in the center.

"The Anawana Tribal Casino," Gunnar said. "And, according to MapQuest, it's one hundred and thirty-seven miles from our front door."

Echolocate *This*

9 Everybody gambles. You don't have to go to a tribal casino to do it either. You do it every day without even realizing it. It could be as simple as skipping your math homework on Tuesday night because you know that your math teacher has cafeteria duty before class on Wednesday, so chances are homework won't be checked, because cafeteria duty will crush the spirit of any teacher.

You gamble when you put off applying for a summer job until July 1—betting that your desire to earn money is outweighed by the fact that you probably won't get the job anyway, so why bother wasting valuable time that could be spent not cleaning your room, or not doing the dishes, or not doing math homework on Tuesday?

The point is, every decision we make is a gamble. My parents are in the middle of a major gamble themselves. They're risking everything on the restaurant. I admire them for it, because they're betting on themselves, which is kind of a noble thing to do. Then, on the other hand, there are the ten lottery tickets my mom buys each week, which are just plain embarrassing.

"What's the point?" my brother Frankie says whenever he sees one lying around. "Do you know scientists have determined that you're more likely to get struck by lightning five times than win?" Which makes me wonder if some poor slob gets his fifth lightning strike every time someone wins the lottery, and how badly do you have to piss off God to be that guy?

"I know the odds are terrible," Mom always says. "But I still get excited. The excitement is worth ten dollars a week."

I guess that's okay—but what happens when ten dollars becomes a hundred? Or a thousand? When does it become a problem? It must happen so slowly, so secretly, that nobody notices until it becomes a terminal illness of its own.

See, my parents can gamble with their restaurant and it's okay, because hard work and talent can change the odds in your favor.

But nothing changes the odds in a casino; they got all these big fancy hotels in Vegas to prove it. The house takes back around 15 percent of all the money gambled, guaranteed. You might win a thousand bucks today and you'll be all excited, totally forgetting that over the past year you lost a lot more than you just won.

Life is kind of like that—I guess Gunnar knew that more than anyone. All our little daily thrills don't change the fact that our chips eventually run out. It's the scalding pot of truth we gotta make tea out of. The tea's pretty good most of the time, unless you're that poor slob who got struck by lightning five times. If you're him, I can't help you, except to point out that your life has the noble purpose of making the rest of us feel lucky.

I didn't know where Mr. Ümlaut was on the lightning-lottery scale, but I had a feeling he was standing in a stormy field, wearing lots of metal.

On Saturday night I was determined to put all the struggles of the Ümlaut family out of my mind entirely. This was to be a night of fun. This was my first date with Kjersten.

Of course we wouldn't be alone—it was a double date with Lexie and Clicking Raoul. Like I said, I couldn't turn down the chance to take Kjersten to a fancy restaurant, and Crawley's was among the fanciest. I was quick to discover that the responsibility of dating an older woman is enough to fry all your brain cells. The logistics alone . . . How are you going to travel? Does she drive you? Is that humiliating if she does? Do you take a bus, and if you do, does that make you seem cheap? Do you call a taxi and go broke from cab fare even before you get where you're going? Or do you walk there together and have everyone snicker at you because she's taller than you?

In the end, I settled for simply meeting her at the restaurant.

My mother raised an eyebrow when I let it slip before I left that Kjersten had a car.

"This girl you're seeing drives?"

"No," I answered. "It's one of those self-driving cars—she just sits there."

My mother is usually pretty quick, but I suppose she didn't

trust her own grasp of changing technology, because she said, "You're kidding, right?" It was very Howie-like. I found that disturbing.

"I'll be home by eleven," I told her as I headed out the front door. "And just in case I'm not, I put the morgue on your speed dial."

"Cut my heart out while you're at it."

"I'll put it on my to-do list."

I made a mental note to actually put the morgue on her speed dial. She'd be mad, but I also knew she'd laugh. Mom and I have a similar sense of humor. I find that disturbing, too.

I arrived ten minutes early, dressed in my best shirt and slacks. Kjersten arrived three minutes late, and was dressed for an evening on the Riviera.

"Is this too much?" she asked, looking at her gown that reflected light like a disco ball. "I heard that Crawley's has a dress code." Don't get me wrong, it wasn't tacky or anything—in fact, it was the opposite. Heads turned when she walked in. I kept expecting flashes from the paparazzi.

"It's perfect," I told her with a big grin. The gown and the way she had put up her hair made her look even older, and I started to imagine us like one of those tests they give little kids. The one that goes: *What's wrong with this picture?* A girl in a gown, crystal chandeliers, a waiter carrying lobsters, and Antsy Bonano. A first grader would pass this test easy.

I greeted her with a kiss on the cheek in clear view of the entire restaurant, in case there was any doubt who she was with.

"You look great," I told her. "But you already know that, right?"

We were seated at a table for four, and I wasn't quite sure whether I was supposed to sit next to her, or across from her, so I sat down first, and let her choose. This was probably the wrong thing to do, because the waiter gave me a look like my mother gives when I do something inexcusable. Then he went to pull out Kjersten's chair for her—clearly what I was supposed to have done.

"I hope you don't mind this double-date thing," I said.

"Just as long as they're not all double dates," she said with a little smile. She reached across the table and took my hand. "I've never been taken on a date to a place this fancy before. You score a ten."

Which meant there was nowhere to go but down.

"Of course," she said . . . a little bit awkwardly, "I've never been on a double date with a blind couple before."

"Don't worry—they're just like people who can see," I told her. "Except that they can't."

"I don't want to say or do anything wrong . . ."

"Don't worry," I told her, "that's *my* department."

Lexie and Raoul arrived a minute or so later, and I wondered where they'd been, since Lexie lives right upstairs, and then I wondered why I'd wondered. I went up to Lexie and took her hand. Kjersten was confused by this, until I guided Lexie's hand into hers. It was something I was just used to doing; it spared Lexie the awkwardness of an inexact docking procedure when it came to shaking hands.

We sat at a table that used to be reserved for famous people from Brooklyn, until they realized that people from Brooklyn who got famous never came back.

Lexie released Moxie, her Seeing Eye dog, from his harness as soon as we sat down, and he obediently took his place beside her chair.

We made awkward small talk for a while about the differences between public high school and their ultra-high-end school for the wealthy blind. For a brief but unpleasant few moments, the girls had this little tennislike discussion about me, like I wasn't there—all I could do was follow the ball back and forth.

"I like Antsy because he's not afraid to say what's on his mind," serves Kjersten.

"Believe me, I know," returns Lexie. "Even when he shouldn't say anything at all."

"Oh, but that's the fun part," Kjersten smashes for the point.

I decided a change in subject matter was called for.

"So," I said to Raoul as the busboy poured water not quite as expertly as I did, "you don't have a guide dog—is that because clicking does it all?"

"Pretty much," said Raoul proudly. "Echolocation makes canes and canine companions seem positively medieval." He'd been pretty quiet until now, but once the conversation became about him, he perked up. "Personally, I think it could be an adaptive trait. Evolutionary, you know?"

"Raoul doesn't have a guide dog because most people don't get them until they're older," Lexie explained curtly. "Technically I'm not supposed to have one either, but you know my grandfather—he pulled some strings."

"I don't need one, anyway," Raoul said. Then he clicked a few times and determined the relative location of our four water glasses, and the fact that mine was only half full, on account of the busboy had run out of water since he didn't check his pitcher the way you're supposed to before you start pouring. And he calls himself a busboy!

"That's amazing!" Kjersten said.

But I wasn't so convinced. "He could have heard the water being poured."

"Could have," Raoul said, "but I wasn't paying attention."

"Okay, then," I said, crossing my arms. "How many fingers am I holding up?"

"He can't be that specific," said Lexie, jumping to his aid, but Raoul clicked, and said: "None. You didn't even put up your hand."

Kjersten looked at me, and grinned.

"All right, Raoul wins," I admitted. "He's amazing."

"And the crowd goes wild!" said Raoul.

"Can we just order?" said Lexie, running her finger across the Braille menu. Maybe it was my imagination, but she was moving her finger a little too fast for her to actually read it. I've seen Lexie read before. I knew the pace of Braille—or at least *her* Braille. Kjersten was watching me watching her, so I looked away. Maybe a double date with Lexie wasn't a good idea after all.

"They're flying me out to Chicago next week," Raoul said. "To do a national talk show."

At that, Lexie closed her menu a little too hard. The sudden clap made Moxie rise to his feet, then sit back down again.

Raoul reached out, gently rubbed his hand along her sleeve, and then took her hand. "What's wrong, baby?"

I grimaced at that. I couldn't help myself. If you knew Lexie Crawley at all, you knew never to call her "baby." That, and the fact that he was holding her hand, just kind of gave me mental dry heaves. I mean, sure, I was dating Kjersten, but I think the human brain isn't designed to deal with situations like this.

I looked over at Kjersten, who noticed my reaction, and again I looked away.

"You don't have to accept all those TV invitations," Lexie told Raoul. "And you don't have to echolocate for people all the time. You're not a sideshow act."

"I don't mind."

"Well, you should."

Suddenly I found my menu to be a place of safety. "I'm thinking maybe the ribs," I said. "How about you, Kjersten?"

"Isn't this a seafood place?"

"Yeah, well, I don't like seafood."

That's when Kjersten's phone rang. Even her ring tone was cool. NeuroToxin's new hit. She pulled the phone out of her purse, looked at the number, then dropped it back in. "Not important," she said, although the look on her face said otherwise.

The waiter took our orders, and once he was gone, small talk became big silence, until Raoul said, "I can echolocate the number of people in the room—wanna see?"

Lexie stood up suddenly. "I need to freshen up." Moxie rose when she did, but she went off without him.

Even though Lexie knew this restaurant inside and out, there were enough people moving around to make navigating to the bathroom like flying through an asteroid field. I got up to escort her.

"I'll be right back," I said to Kjersten, who smiled at me politely. "I gotta go to the bathroom anyway."

As Lexie and I neared the restroom, I heard Kjersten's phone ring again. I glanced back just long enough to see her answer it.

"I like Raoul," I told Lexie. "He's kinda cool."

"If he ever stops talking about himself." We were at the restroom doors, but Lexie didn't make a move to go in. "Having a special ability is all fine and good. But there's got to be more to a person than sonar."

"Yeah . . . I guess if he didn't have that, he'd be pretty boring, huh." I thought about how the conversation was all about him and his uniqueness back at the table, and I realized it wasn't because he was conceited; it was because he had nothing else to talk about.

"Kjersten seems very nice," Lexie said. "I'm happy for you . . ." I knew Lexie well enough to know there was an implied "but" at the end of that sentence. I waited for the but to present itself.

"But . . . there's something about her," Lexie finally said. "I don't know, it's not quite right."

"You barely said a word to each other—how can you tell anything?"

"I have a sense about these things."

"Being blind doesn't make you psychic," I said, sounding more annoyed than I intended to. No—actually I intended to sound exactly like that.

"There's something in her tone of voice," Lexie said, "something in the silences. It's . . . *off*."

"So what? She's got family stuff going on, that's all," I said. "Her brother's illness."

"That may be part of the reason."

"The reason for what?"

"For why she's going out with you."

I didn't like the way this conversation was heading. "Maybe she just likes me—did you ever think of that?"

"Yes, but *why* does she like you?"

"Why does she need a reason? She just does! What—you think it's strange that a girl who's two years older than me, really smart, and looks like a supermodel would want to date me?" There are some things you just shouldn't say out loud. "Okay, maybe it *is* strange. But what's wrong with that? So she's strange. So am I—so are you—since when was there a law against that?"

"Maybe it's not you she likes. Maybe it's the *idea* of you."

"Yeah?" I said. "Well, maybe you should take the *idea* of yourself into that bathroom, because I don't want to talk to you anymore."

She stormed into the bathroom without anyone's help, and with the grace of someone who knew exactly where they were going. Any human asteroid in her way had better watch out. Well, I wasn't going to walk her back. I pulled aside the bus-boy who couldn't pour water right and told him to escort Miss Crawley back to the table when she was done.

She was jealous. That was it. Had to be. Just like I was jealous of her and her clicking celebrity boyfriend. But that would pass. Things were just getting started between Kjersten and me, and I wasn't going to let Lexie ruin it.

When I got back to the table, Kjersten was putting on her coat.

"What's the matter? You cold?"

"I'm sorry, Anthony. I've got to go."

My first response was to look at Raoul. "What did you do?" I asked, figuring maybe he clicked her cleavage, and told her the size of her bra.

"Nothing," said Raoul. "She had a phone call."

"It was my father. I'm grounded."

I just looked at her for a while in stunned denial, like the time I was a kid and my mother told me we're not going to Disney World, on account of the airline suddenly decided to go out of business.

"What? You can't get grounded in the middle of a date. That's like . . . that's like against the law."

"I was grounded *before* the date," she admitted. "I'm not supposed to be out, but my mom doesn't care, and my dad wasn't home."

"Exactly—he's never home, so that voids the grounding, right?"

"He's home now." She zipped up her jacket, sealing away the view of her amazing dress from me and the paparazzi.

"Can't you be like . . . rebellious or something?"

"I *was* rebellious—that's why I'm grounded."

I found myself wondering what she had done, and coming up with things that were probably much more exotic than what really happened. Then I said in a voice far more whiny than I meant it to be, "Can't you be rebellious with *me*?"

She looked at me, and I could tell that she really did want

to stay. But I could also tell from that look that she wouldn't. Then she kissed me, and by the time I recovered from the kiss, she was gone. The waiter, totally clueless, brought the meals and set them down, but right now it was just me and Raoul—and it was anyone's guess if Lexie would come out of the bathroom after what I said to her.

I sat down, dazed by the crash-and-burn of it all, and Raoul says, "So do you want me to echolocate the number of people in the room, or not?"

Collateral Damage, Relative Humidity, and Lemon Pledge in the Dust Bowl of My Life

10 I want to make it absolutely clear that what happened to Gunnar's neighbors was an accident—and for once, I get to share the blame with someone else.

With our dust-bowl due date just a few days away, Gunnar and I were under a time constraint, and we were working too hard on this Steinbeck project to get marked down for being late. I have experience in that department, and know for a fact that there are teachers who measure lateness in microseconds on that world clock they got in England. And there's no bottom to this pit. I actually once got a Z-minus on a late paper. I pointed out to the teacher that she coulda marked me even lower if she used the Russian alphabet, on account of it has something like thirty-three letters instead of twenty-six. She was impressed enough by the suggestion that she raised my grade to a Z-plus.

To avoid letter grades in the lower half of the alphabet, Gunnar and I needed to kill off the plants quickly to get our dust bowl rolling, so we used a lot of herbicide. Now Gunnar's next-door neighbors were all ticked off because their yards were smelling like toxic waste. It was Sunday morning. The day after my not-quite-a-date with Kjersten. I really didn't want to be there and have to face Mr. Ümlaut, who I held personally responsible for ruining my evening. And I didn't want to face Kjersten just yet, because it was too soon after the walkout. But I had to go through the house to get to the backyard. I was hoping Gunnar would answer the door, but he was already working out back.

Kjersten answered the door.

"Hi."

"Hi."

"Nice day."

"Sunny."

"Sun's good."

"Yeah."

"Anyway . . ."

"Right."

I tried to put an end to the misery by moving toward the back door, but she wasn't letting me. Not yet.

"Sorry about last night," she said. "We'll do it again, okay?"

"Yeah, sure, no problem."

"No," she said. "I mean it."

And I could tell that she really did mean it. Deep down, I had kind of felt that a ruined evening meant ruined hopes. It was good to know that another, better date was still on the horizon.

"When's your grounding over?" I asked.

"As soon as I get the grade back on my chemistry test tomorrow—and my father can see I didn't need to skip my tennis tournament to study."

I smiled. "And here I thought you cut school for a wild ski trip." Which was one of my tamer scenarios. I took her hand and stood there for a long moment that, believe it or not, didn't feel awkward at all, then I went out to the backyard.

There was all this cardboard in the yard, because today's project was a cardboard shack for Steinbeck's starving farmers. At the moment I arrived in our little dust bowl, Gunnar was being scolded by his next-door neighbor over the fence. "Look what you've done to my yard! It's all dead!"

"It's that time of year," I offered, pointing out the dead leaves around her yard. "That's why they call it 'fall.'"

"Oh yeah?" she said. "What about the evergreens?"

She indicated some bushes way across the yard that had gone a sickly shade of brown. Then she looked bitterly down at some thorny, leafless bushes in front of her that could have just been dormant if we didn't already know better—because if the herbicide had made it all the way across the yard, these nearby bushes were history.

"Do you have any idea how long I've cultivated this rose garden?"

My next response would have been a short and sweet "Oops," but Gunnar has last week's vocabulary word, which I lack: eloquence.

"'Only when the Rose withers can the beauty of the bush be seen,'" he told her. It shut her up and she stormed away.

"What does that even mean?" I asked after she was gone.

"I don't know, but Emily Dickinson said it."

I told him that quoting Emily Dickinson was just a little too weird, and he agreed to be more testosterone-conscious with his quotations. He looked over at the neighbors' yard, surveying the ruins of the garden. "A little death never hurt anyone," he said. "It gives us perspective. Makes us remember what's important."

I hadn't been too worried about the about the neighbors' plants dying until now. Collateral damage, right? Only this was more than just collateral damage—and only later did we realize why. See, guys all have this problem. It's called the we-don't-need-no-stinkin'-directions problem. Gunnar and I had bought half a dozen jugs of herbicide, coated the plants with the stuff like we were flocking Christmas trees, and we were satisfied with the results. We could have done a commercial for the stuff . . . However, if we had read the directions, we would have seen that the stuff was concentrated—you know, like frozen orange juice: we were supposed to use one part herbicide to ten parts water. So basically we sprayed enough of the stuff to kill the rain forests.

Now all the lawns around Gunnar's house, front and back, were going a strange shade of brown that was almost purple. Our dust bowl was spreading outward like something satanic.

When I got home, my mom wasn't with my dad at the restaurant, like she usually is on Sunday afternoons. She was home, cleaning. This was nothing unusual—but the sheer intensity of the scouring had me worried—like maybe the toxic mold was back, and this time it was personal.

Turns out, it was worse.

"Aunt Mona is coming to visit," Mom told me.

I turned to my sister Christina, who sat cross-legged on the couch, either doing homework or trying to levitate her math book. "No—tell me it's not true!" I begged.

Christina just lowered her eyes and shook her head in the universal this-patient-can't-be-saved gesture.

"How long?"

"How long till she comes, or how long will she stay?" Christina asked.

"Both."

To which Christina responded, "Next week, and only God knows."

It's always that way with Aunt Mona. Her visits are more like wartime occupations. She's the most demanding of our relatives—in fact, we sometimes call her "relative humidity," on account of when Mona's around, everybody sweats. See, Aunt Mona likes to be catered to—but lately the only catering Mom and Dad have been able to do is of the restaurant variety. Plus, when Aunt Mona arrives, all other things manage to get put on hold, and we're all expected to "visit" with her while she's here—especially those first couple of days. With the dust bowl due, tests in every class before Christmas vacation, another date to schedule with Kjersten, and Gunnar's illness hovering like a storm, Aunt Mona was the last thing I needed.

Just so you know, Aunt Mona's my father's older sister. She has a popular business selling perfume imported from places

I've never heard of, and might actually be made up—and she always wears her own perfume. I think she wears them all at one once, because whenever she visits, I break out in hives from the fumes, and the neighborhood clears of wildlife.

She's very successful and business-minded. Nothing wrong with that—I mean, my friend Ira's mom is all hard-core business, and she's a nice, normal, decent human being. But Aunt Mona is not. Aunt Mona uses her success in cruel and unusual ways. You see, Aunt Mona isn't just successful, she's *More Successful Than You,* whoever you happen to be. And even if she's not, she will find a way to make you feel like the pathetic loser you always feared you were, deep down where the intestines gurgle.

Aunt Mona works like 140-hour weeks, and frowns on anyone who doesn't. She has a spotless high-rise condo in Chicago, and frowns on anyone who doesn't. In fact, she spends so much time frowning and looking down her nose at people, she had a plastic surgeon change her nose and Botox her frown wrinkles.

It goes without saying, then, that Aunt Mona is the undisputed judge of all things Bonano—even though she changed her name to Bonneville because it sounded fancier, and because Mona Bonano sounded too much like that "Name Game" song. I'm sure as a kid she was constantly teased with "Mona-Mona-bo-bona, Bonano-fano-fo-fona." And as if Bonneville wasn't snooty enough, she added an accent to her first name, so now it's not Mona, it's Moná. I refuse on principle to ever pronounce it "Moná," and I know she resents it.

It turns out that Aunt Mona was considering moving her

entire company to New York, so she was going to be here for a while. She could, of course, afford one of those fancy New York hotels, where the maids clean between your toes and stuff, but there's this rule about family. It's kind of like the Ten Commandments, and the Miranda rights they read you when you get arrested: Thou shalt stay with thy relatives upon every visit, and anything you say can and will be used against you for the rest of your life.

So Mom's Lemon Pledging all the dining-room furniture until the wood shines like new, and she says to me, "You gotta be on your best behavior when Aunt Mona comes."

"Yeah, yeah," I tell her, having heard it all before.

"You gotta treat her with respect, whether you like it or not."

"Yeah, yeah."

"And you gotta wear that shirt she gave you."

"In your dreams."

Mom laughed. "If that shirt's in my dreams, they'd be nightmares."

I had to laugh, too. The fact that Mom agreed with me that the pink-and-orange "designer" shirt was the worst piece of clothing yet devised by man somehow made it okay to wear it. Like now it was an inside joke, instead of just an ugly shirt.

I picked up one of her rags and polished the high part of the china cabinet that she had trouble reaching. She smiled at me, kinda glad, I guess, that I did it before she asked.

"So, do I gotta wear the shirt in public?"

"No," she says. "Maybe," she adds. "Probably," she concludes.

I don't argue, because what's the use? When it comes to Aunt Mona, the odds of walking away a winner are worse than at the Anawana Tribal Casino. Anyway, I suppose wearing the shirt was better than Mom and Christina's fate. They'd have to wear one of Aunt Mona's perfumes.

Right around then the doorbell rang, and Mom looked up at me with wide eyes and froze. I know what she was thinking. Aunt Mona never showed up when scheduled. She would come early, she would come late, she would come on a different day altogether. But a whole week early?

"Naa," I said to Mom. "It couldn't be."

I went to answer it, fully prepared for a blast of flesh-searing fragrance. But it wasn't Aunt Mona—instead it was two kids—fourth or fifth graders by the look of them, holding out pieces of paper to me.

"Hi, we're collecting spare time for a kid who's dying or something—would you like to donate?"

"Let me see that!" I snatched one of the papers from them. It was my own blank contract—second- or third-generation Xerox, by the look of it. Someone had taken one of my official contracts and was turning out counterfeits!

"Where'd you get this? Who said you could do this?"

"Our teacher," said one kid.

"Our whole class is doing it," said the other.

"So are you going to donate, or what?"

"Get lost." I slammed the door in their faces.

So now collecting for Gunnar had become a school fund-raiser. I felt violated. Cheated. Betrayed by the educational system.

I didn't bother my parents with this—they had enough on their minds, and they'd probably just say "So what?" and they'd be right. It was petty and dumb to think that I owned the whole idea . . . but the thing is, I liked being the Master of Time. Now there were people running around, doing it on their own, without official leadership. They call that anarchy, and it always leads to things like peasants with pitchforks and torches burning things down.

"Think of those little kids as disciples," Howie said, when I mentioned it to him the next day. "Jesus' disciples did all the work for him after he wasn't around no more."

"Yeah, well, I'm still here—and besides, Jesus *knew* his disciples."

"That's only because the lack of technology in those days forced people to have to know each other. Now, because of computers, we really don't gotta know anybody, really."

Then he went on about how today the Sermon on the Mount would be a blog, and the ten plagues on Egypt would be reality TV. None of this addressed the issue, so I told Howie I was leaving, but by all means he should continue the conversation without me.

I think this whole prickly, offended feeling was the first warning. I was sensing things getting out of control—not just out of MY control, but out of control in general. My little idea of giving Gunnar a month to make him feel better was now turning into a monster. And everyone knows what they do to monsters. It's pitchforks and torches again. That happens, see, because people think the monster's got no soul.

As it turns out, they'd be right this time. My monster didn't have a soul . . . and I was about to find that out.

It's Amazing What You Can Get for $49.95

11 There's this junkyard off of Flatlands Avenue where they salvage anything they can from junked cars and dump the cars into massive piles before crushing them into metal squares about the size of coffee tables. It's the kind of place you might invent in a dream, although in a dream, the metal squares would talk to you, on account of they'd be haunted by the people who got murdered and thrown into the trunk before the car got crushed.

Gunnar and I went there looking for rusty engine parts to put in a corner of our dust bowl, to add to the atmosphere of despair.

I did most of the looking, because Gunnar was absorbed in the catalog he was reading. "What do you think of this one?" he said to me while I was looking at a pile of bumpers too modern for our purposes. I didn't look at the catalog because I didn't want any part of it.

"Tell you what. Why don't you make it a surprise?"

"Come on, Antsy, I need your opinion. I like this white one, but it's a little too girlie. And then this one—I don't know, the wood looks like my kitchen cabinets. That just feels weird."

"It *all* feels weird," I told him.

"It must be done."

"So let someone else do it. Why should you care? You're gonna be inside it, you're not gonna be looking at it."

Now he was getting all miffed. "It's about the image I want people to be left with, why can't you understand that? It needs to express who I was, and how I want to be remembered. It's about image—like buying your first car."

I glanced at the catalog and pointed. "Fine—then go with the gunmetal-gray one," I said, fairly disgusted. "It looks like a Mercedes."

He looked at it and nodded. "Maybe I could even put a Mercedes emblem on it. That would be cool."

The fact that Gunnar could discuss coffins like it was nothing didn't just freak me out, it made me angry. "Can't you just pretend like everything's okay and go about your life, like normal dying people?"

He looked at me like there was something wrong with me instead of him. "Why would I want to do that?"

"You're not supposed to be enjoying it. That's all I'm trying to say. Enjoy *other* stuff . . . but don't enjoy . . . that."

"Is it wrong to have a healthy attitude about mortality?"

Before I can even deal with the question, I hear from behind me—

"Yo! Dudes!"

I turn to see a familiar face coming out from behind a pile of taillights. It's Skaterdud. He gives me his official Skaterdud handshake, which I've done enough to actually remember this time. He does it with Gunnar, who fakes his way through it convincingly.

"D'ya get my kick-butt donation?" Skaterdud asks.

"Huh?" says Gunnar, "Oh, right—a whole year. That was very cool."

"Liquid nitrogen, man. We're talking freeze-your-head-till-they-can-cure-you kind of cool, am I not right?"

"No . . . I mean yes. Thank you."

"Hey, ever consider that, man—the deep freeze? Cryonics? I hear they got Walt Disney all frozen underneath the Dumbo ride. The chilliest place on earth, right? Gotta love it!"

"Actually," I said, "that's made up."

"Yeah," admitted Skaterdud, "but don't you wish it wasn't?"

It's then that I realize that I am the gum-band of sanity between these two jaws of death. On the one hand there's Gunnar, who has made dying the focus of his life, and on the other hand, there's Skaterdud, who sees his fatal fortune as a ticket to three carefree decades of living dangerously.

Suddenly I wanted to be anywhere else but in the mouth of madness.

"Listen, Skaterdud, I got somewhere I gotta be," which was true—and for once I was grateful I was needed to pour water at my dad's restaurant. "Do you know where we could find car parts so old and cruddy nobody actually wants them?"

Turns out Skaterdud knew the salvage yard well—his dad was the guy who crushed cars.

"Go straight, and turn left at the mufflers," he told us. "Best be careful. Ain't no rats don't got steroid issues around here. We're talking poodle-sized, *comprende*?"

"Rats don't bother me," Gunnar said.

I, on the other hand, have no love of furry things with non-furry tails. As I rummaged through the appropriate junk pile, afraid to put my hand in any dark hole, I began to wonder if I'd be more like Gunnar or Skaterdud if I knew the time of my final dismissal. Would all of life's dark holes seem insignificant?

"You're right," Gunnar said out of nowhere. He put down his catalog and reached deep into the pile of junk to dislodge a truck piston. "I'll go for the gunmetal-gray coffin. It's classier."

Maybe it's just me, but I'd rather be scared of rat holes than not care.

As Gunnar went off in search of boxes we could carry the stuff in, Skaterdud called me aside and waited until Gunnar was too far away to hear.

"Something ain't wrong about that friend of yours," said the Dud.

I was a little too tired to decipher dud-ese right now, so I just shrugged.

"No, you gotta listen to me, because I see things."

That didn't surprise me entirely. "What kinds of things?"

"Just things. But it's more the things I *don't* see that's got my neck hairs going porcupine on me." Then he looked off after Gunnar again, shaking his head. "Something ain't wrong about him at all—and if you ask me, he's got iceberg written all over him."

We rode home from the junkyard in a public bus, carrying heavy boxes of car parts that greased up the clothes of anyone who passed. We didn't say much, mostly because I was thinking about what Skaterdud had said. Talking to the Dud was enough to challenge anyone's sanity, but if you take the time to decode him, there's something there. The more I thought about it, the more I got the porcupine feeling he was talking about—because I realized he was right. It had to do with Gunnar's emotional state. It had to do with grief. All this time I was explaining away Gunnar's behavior, as if it was all somehow normal under the circumstances, because, face it, I've never been around someone who's got an expiration date before. There was no way for me to really gauge what was standard strangeness, and what was not.

But even I had heard about the five stages of grief.

They're kind of obvious when you think about them. The first stage is denial. It's that moment you look into the goldfish bowl that you haven't cleaned for months and notice that Mr. Moby has officially left the building. You say to yourself, *No, it's not true! Mr. Moby isn't floating belly-up—he's just doing a trick.*

Denial is kinda stupid, but it's understandable. The way I see it, human brains are just slow when it comes to digesting really big, really bad hunks of news. Then, once the brain realizes there's no hurling up this double whopper, it goes to stage two. Anger.

Anger I can understand.

How DARE the universe be so cruel, and take the life of a helpless goldfish!

Then you go kick the wall, or beat up your brother, or do whatever you do when you get mad and you got no one in particular to blame.

Once you calm down, you reach stage three. Bargaining.

Maybe if I act real good, put some ice on my brother's eye, clean the fishbowl and fill it with Evian water, heaven will smile on me, and Mr. Moby will revive.

Ain't gonna happen.

When you realize that nothing's going to bring your goldfish back, you're in stage four: sadness. You eat some ice cream, put on your comfort movie. Everybody's got a comfort movie. It's the one you always play when you feel like the world is about to end. Mine is *Buffet of the Living Dead*. Not the remake, the original. It reminds me of a kinder, simpler time, when you could tell the humans from the zombies, and only the *really* stupid teenagers got their brains eaten.

Once the credits roll, and you've completed stage four, you're ready for stage five. Acceptance. It begins with a flush, sending Mr. Moby the way of all goldfish, and ends with you asking your parents for a hamster.

So I'm sitting there on the bus holding car parts while Gunnar's browsing through his catalog again, and I suddenly realize exactly what Skaterdud meant.

Gunnar never faced stages one through four.

He went straight to acceptance. This crisis, which would have thrown most people's worlds into a tailspin, instead left Gunnar in a perfect glide. There was something fundamentally wrong about things being so "right" with Gunnar. So maybe, as Skaterdud suggested, Pulmonary Monoxic Systemia was just the tip of this iceberg.

Gunnar and I invited our whole English class to our dust bowl for dinner a few nights later, promising "authentic dust-bowl cuisine." Since everyone knew my dad had a restaurant, more than a dozen people actually showed—including our teacher, so we were able to present our report right there. We served everyone a single pea on dusty china, to emphasize what it meant to be hungry in 1939. Our classmates thought we were jerks, but Mrs. Casey appreciated the irony. People kept asking what the faint chemical smell was, and I kept looking to the sky, praying for rain, probably looking like one of Steinbeck's characters—although I wasn't interested in making the corn grow, I just wanted the herbicide to wash away. Gunnar gave the verbal presentation, and I handed Mrs. Casey the written contrast between the book and the movie. She said we did a credible job, which, I guess is better than incredible, because we got an A. I wonder what she would have said if she saw Gunnar's unfinished gravestone, which I forced him to cover with a potato sack before anyone showed up. When she gave back the written report, it came with a contract for two months, signed, witnessed, and stapled to the back of the report.

I went to my computer that night to escape thinking too much, or at least to force myself to think about things that didn't matter. See, when you're on the computer, you get really good at what they call multitasking, and usually the tasks you have to multi are so pointless you can have endless hours without a single useful thought. It's great.

So I'm chatting online with half a dozen people, trying to maintain all these conversations while simultaneously trying to read all these e-mails filled with OMGs and LOLs that aren't even F, while attempting to delete the obvious spam, like all those people in Zimbabwe who have like fourteen million dollars to give me, and the e-mails offering pills "guaranteed" to enlarge your muscles and other things.

Anyway, there I am, sorting online crud, when I notice something I rarely give any attention to: the ad banner at the bottom of the screen. Usually those ad banners are bad animations that say things like SHOOT THE PIG AND QUALIFY FOR OUR MORTGAGE. I've never lowered myself to shooting the pig. But right now the only thing on that banner was a single question, in bright red.

WHAT'S WRONG WITH YOU?

I think I must have seen this one before but it was all subliminal and stuff, because there are many times I'm sitting at this computer asking myself that same question. Meanwhile, all the chats are demanding responses. Ira's is on top. At first he was trying to convince me about how old movies are better than new ones. He's gotten snooty all of a sudden that way, and anytime you're over his house, he forces you to watch classic movies like *Casablanca* and *Alien*. After chatting for like half an hour, he's gotten tired of movie talk, and now he's just telling dead-puppy jokes. This is where things go with Ira, no matter how snooty he pretends to be. I ignore it, and keep my eyes on the ad. Now the answer dances across the banner to join the question.

WHAT'S WRONG WITH YOU?
ASK DR. GIGABYTE!

At first I just chuckled. Everything's a website now. It was the next line that really got me.

WITH DR. G, DIAGNOSIS IS FREE!

I sat there staring and blinking, and shaking my head. Gunnar's doctor was also a "Dr. G." I figured it was just a coincidence. It had to be. I mean, one out of every twenty-six doctors would be Dr. G, right? Well, not exactly, but you know what I mean.

A scoop of ice cream, some root beer, and a dead puppy, Ira's instant message says. He's waiting for my LOL, but right now I've got bigger puppies to fry.

RU still there?

BRB, I type.

I keep wanting to ignore the Dr. G thing, but I can't. It's stuck in my head now.

Maybe it's legitimate, I tried to tell myself. Maybe it's just a real, live doctor who does online consultations.

What did one dead puppy say to the other dead puppy?

I don't care, I answered. *GTG. TTYL,* I told him, and then I added, *IGSINTDRN.* I closed the IM window, taking a little pleasure in the fact that Ira would spend hours trying to figure out what that meant.

I watched a string of other ad banners. Singing chickens, man-eating french fries, aliens in drag. I have no idea what they were all advertising, and I really don't want to know. Then the ad for Dr. G came back. *WHAT'S WRONG WITH YOU?* I clicked on the ad.

It took me to a very professional-looking page that asked me to enter my symptoms. Did I have symptoms? Well, I was overdue for new shoes, and the ones I had were too small, so my toes have been hurting. I entered *Toes hurt.* Then it asked me about twenty other questions, all of which I answered as honestly as I could.

> **Are your toes discolored?**
> No.
> **Do you live in a cold climate?**
> Yes.
> **Are your ankles swollen?**
> No.
> **Have you been bitten by a rodent?**
> Not to my knowledge.

When all the questions had been answered, the website made me wait for about a minute, my anticipation building in spite of myself, and then it gave me a bright blinking diagnosis.

> **You may be suffering from rheumatic gout**
> **complicated by lead poisoning.**
> **To avoid amputation or death, seek a full diagnosis,**
> **available here for $49.95.**
> **All major credit cards accepted.**

When I clicked *no thanks* it took me to a screen that offered pills to relieve my symptoms, which also had the favorable side effect of enlarging muscles and other things.

I tried it three more times. My growling stomach was intestinal gangrene. The crick in my neck was spinal meningitis. The tan line from my watch was acquired melanin deficiency. All could be further diagnosed for $49.95, and all could be treated with the same pills.

I did a lot of pacing that evening. So much that Christina, buried in her homework, actually noticed.

"What's up with you?" she asked as I paced past her room.

I considered telling her, but instead I just asked, "Have you ever heard of Dr. Gigabyte?"

"Yeah," she said. "It told me my zit was late-stage leprosy."

And, grasping at my last straw of reason, I asked, "What if it is?"

"Please, God, let it be true," Christina said. "Because a leper colony would be better than this." Then she turned her attention back to her math book.

There are no words to describe the muddy mix of things you feel the moment you realize your friend probably isn't dying, but instead is conning you. It means that no matter how much you thought you knew him, you don't know him at all.

I still had no proof, only suspicion—after all, Gunnar really could have a different Dr. G—but I had a gut feeling that was impossible to ignore. The more I thought about it, the more certain I was. If Gunnar wasn't dying, it would go a long way to explaining his family's behavior. The way they never talked about it, as if . . . well, as if it wasn't actually happening. And what about Kjersten? Was Kjersten in on this? Could she be? I suppose I could wrap my mind around Gunnar pretending to be sick—but I couldn't believe Kjersten would be in on it, too. It made me realize I didn't know, or understand, her all that well either.

I truly hoped his illness was fake. I'd be relieved if it was—and yet at the same time, the thought was already making me mad. See, I had wasted all that time collecting months for him, thinking I was doing something noble—something that might make his limited time a little brighter—and he accepted those months without the slightest hint of the lie. If this was a con, then everyone had been taken in—there was even that stupid time thermometer by the main office. Sure, I'd be thrilled to know he wasn't dying—but I couldn't deny the dark river of anger running beneath it. Just the right conditions for a sinkhole.

Repossession Is Nine-tenths of the Law,
The Other Tenth Is Not My Problem

12 Mr. Ümlaut was home that night. I had hoped he wouldn't be, because his presence added an even greater air of tension. His Lexus was in the driveway, but not for much longer, because it was being hooked up to a tow truck.

Good, I thought. *If his car is in the shop, maybe he won't go running off to that casino as much.*

He stood there in an undershirt, in spite of the cold, watching his car as it was raised. His hands were in his pockets, and his shoulders slumped.

"Hi," I said awkwardly. "I need to talk to Gunnar."

"Yeah, yeah—he's inside."

He didn't look at me when he spoke, or take his hands out of his pockets, and I got the feeling that if I had asked to see Attila the Hun, his response would have been, "Yeah, yeah—he's inside."

The front door was open a crack. I pushed it all the way

open and stepped inside. Gunnar and Kjersten were in the living room—Gunnar was listening to an iPod so loudly I could hear the song all the way across the room. Kjersten sat on the sofa—but not in the way you usually sit on a sofa—she was sitting stiff and straight, like it was a hard chair. All at once I recognized this scene. This was the aftermath of a family fight. Mrs. Ümlaut was nowhere to be seen, but I suspected she was either upstairs in a room with the door locked, or in the basement violently doing laundry, or somewhere else where she could be alone with whatever emotions had gotten stirred. I wondered if this had anything to do with the car breaking down.

Kjersten noticed me first, but she didn't smile and say hello. In fact, she didn't seem happy to see me at all. Under the circumstances, I wasn't entirely thrilled to see her either, but I told myself not to judge things until I had all the facts.

"Hi," I said, trying to sound as casual as humanly possible, "what's up?"

"Antsy, this isn't a good time."

Well, call me callous, but I had a mission today and would not be put off by a family squabble. "Yeah, but I need to talk to your brother," I told her.

"Please, Antsy—just come back later, okay?"

"This can't wait."

Kjersten gave a resigned sigh, then threw a sofa pillow at Gunnar, getting his attention. He saw me and took off his earphones.

"Good, you're just in time to witness this pivotal moment of our family's history," said Gunnar, seeming resigned, disgusted, amused, and angry all at the same time—a combination of emotions I usually associate with Old Man Crawley. "Have a seat, and enjoy the show," he said. "You want me to get you some popcorn?"

Kjersten threw another pillow at him. "You're *such* an idiot!"

"I'm here to talk about Dr. G," I said, cutting to the chase. "Or should I say, Dr. Gigabyte?"

Then his cool expression hardened until he looked like a stubble-free version of his father. That's when I knew my suspicions were right. It was all there in that look on his face. "There's nothing to talk about," he said.

"I think there is."

He pushed past me. "Talk all you want to Kjersten—I'm sure you'd much rather talk to her anyway." And he was gone, bounding up the stairs. A second later I heard a door slam.

I turned to Kjersten, but she wouldn't look at me. Not that she was intentionally ignoring me, but she clearly had bigger things on her mind at the moment. Personally, I didn't think a family argument was bigger than her brother faking a terminal illness. It occurred to me that in my conversation with Gunnar, I never asked him the question directly. The answer was heavy in the air, but the question needed to be asked.

"Gunnar isn't really sick, is he?"

She looked at me for the first time since I had been alone with her. It was an odd look. I didn't understand it. She seemed bewildered.

"You're joking, right?"

"So . . . then he's actually sick?"

"Of course not!" She took a moment to gauge my seriousness, and her expression became a bit worried. "You mean you didn't know?"

That threw me for a loop. I stammered a bit, and finally shut my mouth long enough to control it and simply said, "No."

"You mean you weren't just humoring him? Playing along?"

"Why would I do that?"

"Because you're a good person."

"I'm not that good!"

"You mean all this time . . . all those contracts . . . you really thought he was dying?" said Kjersten. "I just thought it was a smart way to force Gunnar to snap out of it, and admit the truth!"

"I'm not that smart!"

She covered her mouth with both hands. "Oh no!" Her entire understanding of the situation was based on the premise that everyone knew Gunnar was faking. Now I could see all her thoughts cascading like dominoes. If I didn't know, then other kids didn't know, which meant the whole school believed Gunnar was dying. The fact that this was news to her made me feel sympathetic, and annoyed at the same time.

"Did you actually think Principal Sinclair was just 'playing along'?"

"Principal Sinclair?"

"Did you think that stupid time thermometer was all part of some practical joke?"

"What thermometer?"

I explained it all to her, because between tennis, debate team, and the static filling her family life, she had missed some crucial things. She never heard my Morning Announcement, never noticed the thermometer. She knew that time donations were pouring in, but she thought it was just from other kids. She had no idea that it had become "official," and that the faculty had begun donating months.

"There was a message on the answering machine, from Sinclair," Kjersten said. "But I erased it before I heard the whole thing—I thought it was one of those school recordings we always get." Which was understandable, since Principal Sinclair did sound like an automated message. I suspected there must have been more messages that Gunnar erased himself, knowing full well they were not recordings.

Then I thought about something Kjersten had said. She thought I was trying to get Gunnar to "snap out of it."

"Does Gunnar actually believe Dr. Gigabyte?" I asked. "Does he really think he's dying?"

The question just frustrated her. "How should I know? You know what he's like—no one can ever figure out what he's really thinking."

I was relieved to know that it wasn't just me. If he stymied his own sister, it meant he was more of a mystery, and I was less of a numbskull.

Out front I heard the scrape of metal on pavement, and glanced out of the window to see the tow truck leaving the driveway, scraping the underside of the Lexus on the curb as it did. Mr. Ümlaut just stood there and watched it go. I almost expected him to wave.

"So what's wrong with your car?" I asked, in an attempt to change the subject.

"It's not our car," Kjersten said. "At least not anymore." Then she got up and closed the blinds so she didn't have to look at her father standing in the driveway. "It just got repossessed."

This is something I knew a little bit about. When my parents got my brother Frankie a car, he was supposed to get a part-time job and make payments on it. He didn't, and the family fights all became about how they'd come and take the car away. Dad was going to let the bank repossess the car to teach Frankie a lesson, but it never got that far—Frankie got the job, started making payments, and the threatening phone calls and letters in red ink stopped coming. I wondered how many letters and phone calls you had to ignore until they actually showed up at your door.

"My father tried to stop them by ripping out some hoses so they couldn't drive it away. Then they sent a tow truck."

"I'm sorry," was all I could say to Kjersten. Now I felt like an idiot for dismissing the whole thing as just a family argument—but before I started beating myself up over it, I did a quick search for ultracool Antsy, who seemed to be easier to find these days. Even without thinking, I knew what he would do. I went to her, and gave her a gentle kiss. She kissed me back with a little bit of spark, so I kissed her again with slightly higher voltage, and she returned that with enough electricity to light Times Square, but before circuit breakers started popping, we shut it down, because we both knew this wasn't the time or place. Just my luck, right?

"Don't be too hard on Gunnar," Kjersten said.

"Hey, you're the one throwing pillows at him."

With a gust of cold air, Mr. Ümlaut came in and saw Kjersten and me standing a little too close. I made no move to back away from her. Sometimes a guy's gotta stand his ground.

"I thought your business was with Gunnar," he said.

"Yeah, well, I got lots of business."

He looked from me to Kjersten, to me again, like he was watching one of her tennis matches. Finally he settled his gaze on her, and he pointed the parental threatening finger.

"We'll talk about this later." Without looking at me again, he went to the back of the house and I heard the door to his study close. This was a house of many closing doors.

"We won't talk," Kjersten said. "He says that all the time, but we never do." Kjersten smiled at me, but there wasn't much joy in that smile.

"Yeah," I said, shaking my head in understanding. "Fathers and follow-through . . ." My own father didn't follow through on much of anything these days—threats *or* promises—since he started the restaurant. But Mr. Ümlaut did not have work as an excuse.

"I just wish things could be the way they were a couple of years ago," Kjersten said, "back when everything was fine—or at least when I was naive enough to think it was." Some warmth came back to her smile as she looked at me. I was glad I could have that effect on her. "You're lucky you're a freshman—you've got your whole life ahead of you."

That made me laugh. "And you don't?"

She kissed me gently on the forehead, then looked out to the grease spot on the driveway where her father's car had been. "My life is going to change very soon."

"Whoever it is, I have no intention of letting you in."

I knocked on Gunnar's door again. A more sensible guy

might have been satisfied with Kjersten's kisses and left, convincing himself that Gunnar was somebody else's problem, but I don't possess the self-preservation instinct. I've got the this-frying-pan-isn't-hot-enough-let's-try-the-fire instinct. I must have been Roadkyll Raccoon in a previous life.

I knocked again. This time there was no response, but I did hear the door being unlocked. I opened it to find Gunnar lying facedown on his bed, with a pillow over his head to shut out the world. This was quite a feat—because just a second ago he had unlocked the door. He must have hurried back to his bed at lightning speed, just so he could present himself to me in this state of anguish.

I sat at his desk chair, realizing he couldn't stay that way for long—he'd have to breathe eventually. Sure enough, he loosened the grip on the pillow, turned to see me for just a split second, then turned his face the other way.

"Go away," he said. But if he really wanted me to go away, he wouldn't have unlocked the door.

I said to him the one thing I could think to say under the circumstances. "I'm sorry you're not dying."

He sat up and faced me. He seemed insulted. "Who says I'm not? Just because it's a Dr. Gigabyte diagnosis doesn't mean it's not true."

"Well, then maybe my sister has leprosy."

He showed no sign of being surprised or confused by that, and I wondered if maybe he had, at some point, been given that diagnosis by Dr. Gigabyte, too.

"Have you seen any real doctors? What do they say?"

"I don't care what they say. *'The enlightened man knows the workings of his own body and soul.'*"

"Who said that?" I asked.

I could see him thinking and he said, "The Dalai Lama."

"You made that up!"

"So what."

And then I had a sudden revelation. "You made them *all* up!" Even as I said it, I knew it was true. Nobody could have so many quotes-for-all-occasions at their fingertips. "None of those people ever said those things, did they? Your quotes are all fake!"

He looked down at the pillow in his hands, and punched it like he was kneading a wad of dough. "That doesn't mean they *couldn't* have said them," he mumbled.

I laughed. Maybe it was the wrong thing to do, but the fact that even his pretensions were pretend struck me as funny. He didn't react well to that. He stood up, and went to the door. "I'd like you to leave now."

This time I think he meant it. "Well, for what it's worth, I'm actually glad you're not dying." I stood up and went to the door. "Do your parents have any idea you've been conning the whole school?"

"I'm not conning anybody," he said. "My life is over. Whether or not I actually die is just a technicality."

But before I could ask him what that meant, he closed the door between us.

The next day—the Friday before a desperately needed Christmas vacation—I was hauled into the principal's office again. This time he already had other guests—a man and a woman in expensive-looking business suits. When I walked in, they both stood up. I flinched, like you do when the cat jumps out in a horror movie.

"Ah," said Principal Sinclair, "here's the boy I've been telling you about." I shook their hands—but can't remember their names, on account of my brain was still processing the fact that they had been talking about me—but I'm pretty sure that the woman was the newly elected superintendent of schools.

"Anthony has been spearheading a schoolwide community-service effort to give hope to a terminally ill student."

"Uh . . . yeah," I said, looking anywhere but at the three of them. "Funny you should mention that . . ."

"I've heard all about it," said the superintendent. "We need more students like you."

That almost made me laugh.

"If you don't mind," the man said, "we'd like to donate time, too."

Call me a gutless wonder, but I didn't have the courage to let them know the truth about Gunnar and his "illness." I tried, but the words stuck in my throat and clung to my tonsils like strep, refusing to come out.

"Yeah, sure, why not," I said, and reached into my backpack, pulling out two blank time contracts for them to fill in and sign, with my principal signing as witness. Then, when it was done, Principal Sinclair sat on the corner of his desk, in that casual I'm-your-principal-but-I'm-also-your-friend kind of way. "Now, I'm sure you've heard that the student council has organized a rally for Gunnar during the first week of January," he said.

"They have?"

"Yes—and I think you should give a speech, Anthony."

There comes a moment in every really, really bad situation when you realize your canoe's leaking, there's no paddle, and you can hear Niagara Falls up ahead. There's nothing you can do but hold on and pray for deliverance. I don't mean the movie *Deliverance,* which is, coincidentally, about canoes—I mean real, Hail Mary, Twenty-third Psalm kind of deliverance.

"I'm not good at speeches."

"I'm sure you'll do fine," said the superintendent. "Just speak from the heart."

And the other guy said, "We'll all be there to support you."

"You'll be there?" I asked. The Falls were getting louder by the minute.

"This school," said the principal, "is under consideration as a National Blue Ribbon school. Academics are only a part of that. The school must also demonstrate that its students are committed to making the world a better place . . . and you, Anthony, are our shining star."

Kidnap Ye Grouchy Gentleman,
with Something to Dismay

13 In spite of what happened on the Double Date From Hell, my friendship with Lexie was back to normal. "I care about you too much to be anything more than mildly furious at you," she had told me, but even then, I could tell she wasn't furious at all.

The two of us kidnapped her grandfather as planned—the first Saturday of Christmas vacation. As usual, Old Man Crawley had no concept of what was in store for him today. "I don't want to do this!" he yelled as I fought to blindfold him. "I'm calling the police! I'll skewer you on the end of my cane!" But this was all part of the ritual.

By the time we got him out to his chauffeured Lincoln, he had stopped complaining about being kidnapped. Now he merely complained about the conditions.

"You forgot my winter coat."

"It's a warm day."

"I just ate. If I have digestive problems because of this, I won't be happy."

"When are you ever happy?" I asked.

"Your attitude does not bode well for your paycheck."

But I knew he paid me for my attitude as well. It was all part of the ambience of the experience.

"This one's special, Grandpa," Lexie assured him.

"That's what you always say," he grumbled.

Our Holiday Kidnapping Extravaganza was a zip line fifty feet off the ground through the treetops of Prospect Park—the largest park in Brooklyn. Lexie had arranged to have engineering students build the zip line for class credit. There were two platforms equipped with rope-and-pulley lift systems, because Old Man Crawley couldn't be expected to climb a ladder. Flying down the wire from one tree to the other, you reached a top speed of about forty miles an hour.

This was a good distraction from the Gunnar Debacle, as I was now calling it, since I figured I'd earned the right to be as pretentious as him. Still, it weighed heavily on my mind.

As the chauffeur drove to Prospect Park, I told Lexie everything.

"I knew it!" she said. "I knew something was wrong with that whole family. I could tell the way whatserface left that night without as much as a good-bye."

"You were pouting in the bathroom," I reminded her. "She couldn't say good-bye to you. And anyway, I'm not breaking up with her, if that's what you're thinking. The problem is with her brother, not her."

I had had enough time to really think about Gunnar's behavior, and realized that this wasn't just a simple con. He wasn't faking in the traditional sense. There's a fine line between being a hypochondriac and being a faker. I think Gunnar was speeding down that particular zip line at speeds in excess of forty miles an hour.

"Sounds to me," said Lexie, "that he's more miserable at the prospect of being healthy than being sick."

"Exactly! It's like he actually wants to have Pulmonary Monoxic Systemia." And I posed to her the question that had been rattling in my head for days. "Why would anyone WANT to be dying?"

"*Munchausen,*" said Lexie.

I was tempted to say "gesundheit," but I took the more serious route instead. "What's that?" I asked. "Sounds bad."

"It can be. It's a mental illness where someone lies about being sick, to get attention. There are people who give themselves infections, so they can go to the doctor. There are people who make their own children sick."

"All for attention?"

"Well," said Lexie, "it's complicated."

"Which means," grumbled her blindfolded grandfather, "that you're wasting your breath trying to explain it to him."

I thought about Gunnar. Did he want attention? He got a lot of it already. He was popular, girls liked him, everyone knew him. He wasn't starving to be noticed . . . but, on the other hand, he wasn't exactly the focus of his parents' lives these days. But, on the other hand, neither was I, and I wasn't telling everyone I had a dreaded disease, although I'm sure there are some people who are convinced I do.

We reached Prospect Park and walked Crawley, still blindfolded, to the first tree. When we took off the blindfold, Crawley made a move to run, but I caught him. This was a standard part of the ritual, too.

"This is too dangerous!" he shouted as we moved him onto a platform rigged with pulleys—probably more than were necessary, but after all, it was done by engineering students—they were trying to show off. "There must be laws against things like this!"

"That'll be a great quote for your tombstone," I said, but then I shut up, because it reminded me of Gunnar.

Crawley gave me the kind of gaze that knows no repeatable words, and we were hoisted up to the high platform, where one of the engineering students waited with sets of harnesses, helmets, and gear that looked like it was meant for space walks.

"How far is it to the other platform?" I asked the engineering guy next to me, but before he could answer, Crawley said bitterly:

"Lexie's boyfriend could probably tell you." And he made some clicking noises.

"Stop it, Grandpa."

Now that he was safely in his harness, I pushed him and he went flying down the zip line, screaming and cursing for all he was worth.

"So how *is* Raoul?" I asked Lexie.

"Raoul and I agreed it was best to end it."

"I'm sorry."

"No you're not."

"Yes, I am," I told her. "Because now you're going to want me to end it with Kjersten, just to keep the status quo."

"Status quo," she said. "Big words for you."

"I'm Catholic," I reminded her. "I get Latin." Then I gave her a gentle shove, and she shot down the zip line, toward her grandfather and the nervous engineering students waiting to catch her.

"It's a quarter mile," said the engineering student, who had been waiting all this time to answer my question, "but it feels a lot longer!"

I pulled up the rear, shouting and whooping as the landscape of Prospect Park shot beneath me. This kidnapping was a winner! The zip line did exactly what it was supposed to do—it filled our senses and souls with excitement. It reminded us what it meant to be alive. For twenty shining seconds there was nothing but me, the wind, and the fifty feet between me and the ground. The engineering guy was wrong. It felt too short!

By the time I arrived, Crawley had already recovered some of his usual demeanor.

"So, whaddaya think?" I asked.

"I'm only mildly impressed." From him, this was a five-star review.

"It was . . . exhilarating," Lexie said. I could tell she hadn't cared for it. When you're flying down a zip line, I suppose sight is a sense worth having.

The students lowered us from the platform, working hard on the pulleys like medieval sailors, and as we descended, Crawley said to me, "As usual, you're missing the obvious."

"Excuse me?"

"With regard to your not-quite-dying friend—you're missing the obvious."

I crossed my arms. "So tell us. We await your brilliance, O Ancient One."

For once he ignored my sarcasm. "It's not that he wants to die—it's that he needs to be sick. The sooner you find out why he needs to be sick, the sooner you can solve this mystery and return to your mediocre existence."

I didn't respond, because as much as I hated to admit it, I knew he was right.

"Now," he said, "take me back to the other tree, so we can do that again."

Crawley contacted the parks department shortly after the kidnapping and offered to build a zip line tourist attraction in Prospect Park. He got the blessing of the city, and wouldn't you know it, the zip line was already in place. Any minute he'll be making a hefty profit from it.

"The difference between you and me," he once told me, "is that when I look at the world, I see opportunity. When you look at the world, you're just trying to find a place to urinate."

When I got home that afternoon, I decided to play Sherlock Holmes and figure out why Gunnar needed to be sick. I did some in-depth research on Pulmonary Monoxic Systemia.

Although the disease is almost always fatal within a year of diagnosis, huge strides were being made in research recently, and there were early reports that test patients were living longer, healthier lives. The leading research and all the hopeful results were coming from Columbia University Medical Center, right in Manhattan.

I thought about Dr. G. The thing with the Dr. G website is that you can throw out the same basic symptoms, and each time it would diagnose you with something else. I wonder how many diagnoses Gunnar had gotten before he convinced himself that this is what he had.

And wasn't it convenient that all the hope for Gunnar's illness lay right here in New York?

Before I could think about it much further, I got a call from my father. He needed me to work at the restaurant. The Crawley kidnapping had exhausted me, and it was the last thing I wanted to do today.

"There are laws against child labor," I told him.

"Aren't you always telling us you're not a child?"

"What about my homework? Is your restaurant more important than my education?"

"It's *our* restaurant, not just mine—and didn't Christmas vacation start today?"

I knew he had me.

I showed up at seven and did my job, but the whole situation with Gunnar never left my mind entirely. Sure, it was vacation, but there was a big fat Gunnar-themed rally waiting for me when vacation was over. I was irritable, but maintained an air of professionalism for most of the evening. Things would have been fine if it hadn't been for the single certified idiot at table number nine.

He arrived at around seven-thirty with a scowling wife, and two kids who wouldn't stop fighting. From the moment he sits down, this guy starts complaining. His fork has spots on it; the wine isn't cold enough. The appetizer came out too late and the main course came out too early. He demands to see the manager, and my father comes over. I'm standing there, refilling water glasses, after having been chewed out by the guy for not having refilled them the instant he took a sip. For him I don't bother with skillful pouring.

"How can you call this a restaurant?" the guy complains while his kids kick each other under the table. "The service is lousy, the food came out cold, and there's a horrible stench in the air."

Well, first of all, the service was perfect, because my mother was his waitress, and she is the queen of quality control. Secondly, I know the food was hot, because I served it myself, and nearly burned my hands on the plate. And third, the horrible stench was coming from his son.

But my dad—he gets all apologetic, offering free dessert, and discounts off the guy's next visit, and such. That just makes me angry. See, my dad used to work in a big corporation, full of guys like this, so he had developed an idiot-resistant personality. I, on the other hand, had not. All I had going for me at the moment was a big pitcher of ice water.

This is why I could never get a job as a busboy in a restaurant my family didn't own . . . because, for the first time in my water-pouring history, I missed the glass. In fact, all the water in the pitcher missed the glass, and found the top of the guy's head instead.

After I was done pouring the pitcher of ice water on him, he finally fell silent, and stared at me in total shock. And I said, "I'm sorry—did you want bottled water instead?"

To my amazement, the rest of the restaurant started applauding. Someone even snapped a picture. I was ready to take a bow, but my father grabbed my arm. He grabbed it hard, and when I looked at him, the expression in his eyes was not one of gratitude. "Wait for me in the kitchen," he growled. Very rarely did my father speak in growls. When he was mad he usually yelled, and that was okay. Speaking in growls was not. I hurried off to the kitchen, sat on a stool, and waited, feeling more like a little kid than I had in years.

Christina came up to me. I don't know if she saw what happened, but I'm sure she guessed the gist. "I made a swan for you," she said, and handed me a folded napkin.

"Thanks," I said. "Got any Himalayan mantras I can recite for the occasion?"

"I'm beyond that now," she told me. "I'm into chakra points." She massaged some spots on my back that failed to relax me, then went to fold more napkins.

Dad did not come back to talk to me at all that night. He just let me stew on the stool. Mom would occasionally pass by to pick up orders and would scowl, shake her head, or wag her finger. Then eventually she gave me a plate of food. That's how I knew Dad was truly, truly angry. If Mom felt sorry enough for me to feed me, it meant I was in a world of trouble.

Eventually Mom just sent me home, because she couldn't stand to see me sitting there so miserably on that stool.

—

Before my parents got home that night, I got a call from Old Man Crawley, who must have had spies in the restaurant again.

"Did you actually pour a pitcher of water over a man's head?" he asked.

"Yes, sir," I replied. I was too exhausted to make excuses.

"And did it feel good to do so?"

"Yes, sir, it did. He was an idiot."

"Was this a premeditated attack on your part?"

"Uh . . . no, sir. It was kind of . . . spontaneous."

He paused for a long time. "I see," he finally said. "You'll be hearing from me." And he hung up. He didn't even bother to torment me with how much I had disappointed him—that's how bad this was. I couldn't help but feel that "you'll be hearing from me" were among the worst possible words to hear at the end of a conversation with Crawley. It was even worse than "you'll be hearing from my attorney."

This water incident might have meant a whole lot of bad things—including retribution against my father somehow—after all, it was Crawley's money that got my dad's restaurant going. Crawley could shut it down with a snap of his fingers, and I wouldn't put it past him to do it.

Dad did not punish me when he got home. He didn't punish me the next day. He just avoided me. It didn't feel like an intentional cold shoulder—it felt more like he was so disgusted, he just didn't want to have anything to do with me. It wasn't until Monday that I found out why.

On Monday the news had a headline that read:

BUSBOY BAPTIZES BOSWELL

And there it was, not on page four of the school paper, but smack on the cover of the *New York Post*—a full-page picture of the idiot from table nine, drenched in water, and me holding the empty pitcher. It was the picture taken by one of the other diners that night.

Getting your picture on the cover of the *New York Post* is never a good thing. It means that you're either a murderer, a murderee, or a humiliated public official. This time it was option three. The idiot from table nine was none other than Senator Warwick Boswell, and I was the one who had humiliated him.

That morning my father was already scouring the classifieds for job opportunities, as if he was expecting the restaurant to shut down in a matter of days.

"Dad, I'm sorry . . ." It was the first time I tried to breach the silence between us, but he put up his hand.

"Let's not do this, okay, Antsy?" He didn't even look up at me.

That's how it was for most of Christmas vacation. And it hurt. See, in our family we fought, we yelled, we gouged at one another's feelings, and then we made up. Our fights were fiery—never cold, and it got me to thinking about what my mom had once said about hell—how it's all cold and lonely.

Now I knew she was right, because I'd rather have fire shooting out of my dad's mouth like a dragon than suffer this nuclear winter.

My dad and I used to be able to talk. Even when something was bad, even when we were ready to strangle each other, we could talk. But not now.

Let's not do this, okay, Antsy?

Entire species died in that kind of cold.

Nobody Likes Me,
Everybody Hates Me,
Think I'll Eat Some Worms

14 Christmas came and went uneventfully, which, considering the previous set of events, was a good thing. For reasons that may or may not have been retribution for missing Thanksgiving, most of our relatives had other plans. We could have gone to Philadelphia to be with Mom's side of the family, but with Aunt Mona coming on Christmas Eve, we had to pass. Then Aunt Mona calls at the last minute to tell us she can't come till after New Year's. Typical.

"It wouldn't be a visit from Mona," Mom said, "if she didn't ruin the plans we made around her."

"She did us a favor," Dad responded, because he was simply too burned out to travel all the way to Philly anyway. Besides, he never spoke out against his sister, no matter what the situation. It was a sore spot with Mom.

"You watch," said Mom, "when she does come, she'll show up without any warning, and expect us to drop everything."

Christmas morning lacked the magic it usually had. At first I thought it was just me getting older, but the more I thought about it, the more I realized that wasn't the case. The tree was trimmed better than ever—but that was just because Christina and I worked hard to make it so. There were fewer presents under the tree, since there wasn't a horde of relatives—but that would have been okay. What really made it hard was that Dad was clearly not present in the moment, as they say. His thoughts were on the restaurant, his future, and I guess our futures, too. He was all preoccupied, and that made Mom preoccupied with him. I could tell that Mom resented the air of anxiety in our lives lately, but still did everything she could to get Dad to relax. I wanted to tell him to just get over it, but how could I? After all, I was the cause of his latest stress bomb.

The day after Christmas I went to give Kjersten her Christmas gift. Was it crazy for me to think we could have a somewhat normal relationship, in spite of all the abnormal stuff around us? Going there didn't feel right. I wasn't ready to face Gunnar—I didn't know how to talk to him, because I knew every word out of my mouth would be another way of asking why. Why did he *need* to be sick? Why did he let it go so far? Why did he have to draw me into it? The Great Gunnar Rally was planned for the day after we got back to school. The speech I was supposed to deliver hung over my head—and I resented Gunnar for putting me in that position.

When I arrived on their street that day, there was no denying the neighborhood's collateral damage. I moved past looming lawns of death, trying to gauge how bad it was. The dust bowl had already spread halfway down the block. All the evergreens were yellow, and everything that should have been yellow was that strange bruise shade of brown. Men were standing out front looking at the devastation, and their wives looked on, watching to see if their men would break.

The only thing green was, ironically, right on the Ümlaut door. A big green Christmas wreath . . . but when I got closer, I could see it was plastic.

Gunnar answered the door.

"I'm here to see your sister," I told him.

He looked at the wrapped package in my hands. "She's upstairs." Then he walked away. I should have let him go, but whether I like it or not, my mouth has a mind of its own.

"You're still not cyanotic," I said to him. "But if it's that important to you, you can buy some blue lipstick and pretend that you are."

He turned to me then. I could tell he was hurt, even though it didn't show in his face. Part of me felt glad about it, and another part of me felt ashamed for saying something so nasty. I found myself mad at both parts.

Gunnar gave me a cold gaze and said, "That would have been much more effective if you bought some for me as a Christmas gift," then he left.

"Wish I had thought of it," I shouted after him. Actually, I *had* thought of it, but I wouldn't sink so low as to get him a cruel gift. Besides, I didn't want to be seen buying blue lipstick. Even if no one saw me, there *are* surveillance cameras.

I found Kjersten up in her room watching *Moëba*, a zany cartoon about ethnically diverse single-celled organisms in Earth's primordial ooze. It seemed odd that she'd be watching this. In fact, she was so absorbed, it took her a moment to notice I was there.

"Antsy!"

"Hi." It came out sounding like a one-word apology.

She stood up and gave me a hug. "You're not having much luck with photographers lately, are you?" I could see the special Antsy edition of the *New York Post* on her desk.

"No," I admitted, "and now there's an animated version on YouTube."

"Could be worse," she said, although downloadable e-humiliation is about as low as it gets.

The moment became awkward, and she glanced back at the TV, where Moëba was punching out a dim-witted paramecium.

"I used to love this show," she said.

"So did I," I told her. "When I was, like, eight."

She sighed. "Things were simpler then." Then she turned off the TV. "So, is that for me?"

"Oh . . . yeah," I said, handing her the gift. "Merry Christmas." Again, I sounded like I was apologizing for something. It was annoying.

"Yours is still under the tree," she said. I hadn't even noticed a tree downstairs.

She opened up her package, to reveal a NeuroToxin jacket.

"It's from their *Bubonic Nights* tour. Look—Jaxon Beale's autograph is embroidered on the sleeve."

"I noticed," Kjersten said. "I love Jaxon Beale!"

In case you've been living on a desert island, Jaxon Beale, former guitarist for Death Crab, is the guitarist *and* lead singer of NeuroToxin.

She thanked me, and put the jacket on. It looked good on her, but then, what didn't? It made me feel good that I could, at least for a few minutes, break her out of a world of repossessed cars, furious neighbors, and a brother on deathwatch.

"You want to do something today?' she asked.

To be honest, I hadn't given the day much thought beyond handing her the jacket. "Sure," I said. "How about a movie?"

"Something funny," she said. "Let's make it something funny."

"Why don't you pick—there's a whole bunch of new movies at the Mondoplex." Then I added, "You can even drive. I'm over that whole macho thing about riding shotgun with my girlfriend."

This was, I realized, the first time I used the word "girlfriend" with her. I watched to see if her reaction would be positive, negative, or neutral. It was negative, but not because of the word "girlfriend." Her problem was with the word "drive."

"We can't drive. My dad borrowed my car this morning."

I wondered if he had borrowed it to go gambling, but decided not to ask. "Your mom could drive us . . ."

"My mom's spending the holiday with family in Sweden, and she parked her car at the airport."

Why, I wondered, would she choose to pay for airport parking instead of just leaving her car for her husband to use? Again, I decided it was best not to ask. The whole family was a can of worms waiting to happen, and I, for one, was not going to supply the can opener.

"Sweden, huh?" I said. "Sounds like fun—why didn't you go with her?"

"It's Sweden, and it's winter—isn't that reason enough?"

"I bet there'd be snow."

"Snow, and ice, and eighteen hours of darkness. I hate it."

"Well, I'm sure it's a whole lot better than Christmas in Brooklyn." She shrugged gloomily, so I tried a different tack. "Well, I'm glad you didn't go, because now we can see each other all vacation."

That made her smile, and it wasn't just a polite smile, it was a real one. I silently reveled in the fact that she actually did want to spend time with me. We bundled up against the windy afternoon, braved the neighborhood dust bowl, and took a bus to the Mondoplex.

For several reasons, I will not give a blow-by-blow description of our darkened-movie-theater experience. First of all, it's none of your business, and secondly, anything you *think* happened is probably better than what actually did.

But for those of you who have never experienced the phenomenon called a movie-theater date, there are a few general things I can tell you:

1. Your hand completely falls asleep after about fifteen minutes around a girl's shoulder, especially if she's taller than you. It's better just to hold hands.

2. While holding hands, you can't manage both a tub of popcorn and a drink. One of them is bound to spill. Pray it's the popcorn.

3. If you ever come within six inches of actually kissing, you will suddenly become more interesting than the movie to the

entire audience, including one creep with a laser pointer, who you'll be ready to kill long before the credits roll.

As for the movie itself, it wasn't the movie I expected Kjersten to choose. I thought Kjersten might pick a love story, or a foreign film or something . . . instead she chose this lowbrow teen comedy that I might have gone to see with Howie and Ira, but never thought I'd see with her. It wasn't even one of the better lowbrow movies either. I mean, I've enjoyed my share of amazingly stupid movies, but this one was so bad, and so unfunny, it was embarrassing. This was a film that would actually insult Wendell Tiggor's "intelligence," and with every dumb, raunchy thing that happened on-screen, I kept expecting her to slap me for the mere fact that I was a guy.

Eighty-six agonizing minutes later, the movie was over and we were walking down the street holding hands—the first time we actually held hands while publicly walking. She didn't quite tower over me, but the difference was enough for me to be self-conscious about it. Every time someone nearby laughed, I involuntarily snapped my head around like maybe it was directed at us. Kjersten had no such worries.

"Did you like the movie?" she asked.

"It was all right, I guess."

"I thought it was funny," she said.

"Yeah." I searched for something worth saying. "When the fat guy got stuck in the Jell-O-filled swimming pool naked, that was funny."

"You didn't like it," she said, reading right through me.

"Well, it's just that . . . I don't know . . . you're on the debate team and everything. I thought you'd want to see a movie that would, uh . . . broaden my horizons."

"I'm happy with your horizons just where they are."

I should have felt good about that. After all, it was unconditional acceptance from my girlfriend . . . but like Gunnar's "acceptance," it was all wrong. Not that I wanted her to go through denial, fear, and anger while dating me—although a little bargaining might be fun. The thing is, I knew she chose the movie because she thought I would like it. What did that say about her opinion of *me*?

Yeah, yeah, I know, guys aren't supposed to think about stuff like that. I should be happy that I'm successfully playing out of my league, batting a thousand, and have earned bragging rights. I guess that was enough at first, but not anymore. I blame Lexie. She was the one who first broadened my horizons.

Kjersten's car was in the driveway when we got home, which meant her father was there. I would have gone in, but Kjersten didn't want to make any waves. She kissed me quickly at the door, ducked inside for a moment, and came out with a long, skinny box, wrapped perfectly, with a golden Christmas bow. "You can open it when you get home," she said. "I hope you'll like it."

And from inside I heard Gunnar shout, "It's a skateboard."

She growled in frustration, and handed me the box, accidentally knocking the wreath off the door. Quickly she scrambled to put it back up, but not quickly enough. I got a clear glimpse of the notice pasted to the front door that had been hidden by the wreath. She knew I saw it—but what could she do? She made sure the wreath was hung firmly on the nail, and pretended it hadn't happened. "See you tomorrow?" she said.

"Yeah . . . Yeah, sure, see you tomorrow."

Before she closed the door, I caught a glimpse of Gunnar

watching me from inside, his eyes filled with fatalistic doom, as unnerving as a dozen dying yards.

It was a nice skateboard. High-quality Spitfire wheels, cool design. I sat on my bed that evening, running my fingers over the grip tape surface, and the smooth polished back. I spun the wheels, and listened to the satisfying clatter of the bearings. It was everything you'd want in a skateboard, except for one thing. I didn't want a skateboard.

See, there's a time for everything in life—and everyone's clock is different. There are guys who use skateboards right up until they get their license—after all, it's a useful mode of transportation. Then there are guys like Skaterdud, to whom skateboarding is like a religion, and they'll do it all their lives. I'm sure the Dud won't just fall off that aircraft carrier, he'll roll off it. But my skateboard phase ended the summer before ninth grade. I kind of outgrew it—and everyone knows the second you outgrow something, it's like poison for a couple of years, until it becomes historically significant in your life and you can look back on it fondly.

It was all starting to make sense now. Especially after seeing that awful notice plastered on their front door.

HOUSE IN FORECLOSURE
RESIDENTS ARE HEREBY GIVEN THIRTY DAYS
TO VACATE PREMISES

It was far worse than any field of doom Gunnar and I had created. Thirty days. How do you cope with the world coming down around you, when your parents just seem to be running away? Is it easier to believe that it's the end of everything rather than face it, and start carving tombstones like Gunnar? Or maybe you just go into full retreat, like Kjersten—who wasn't interested in bringing me up to her level, but rather wanted to come down to mine—or at least what she *thought* was my level. Dumb movies, cool skateboards, and awkward fourteen-year-old advances. Because "things were so much simpler then."

Lexie had been right. Kjersten was dating "the idea" of me.

Could I be what Kjersten needed? Did I want to be? As I sat there running my hands along the edge of the skateboard, I realized that the Ümlaut can of worms was a big old industrial drum, and I was already inside, eating worms left and right.

What the Ümlauts really needed was time—and not the kind I could print out of my computer, but *real* time. And as for Kjersten, if I really cared about her—and I did—I realized the best I could do was to become "the idea of me" as much as possible for her. I couldn't give her time, but maybe I could give her a little time travel.

So I got on that skateboard and rode it around and around and around, trying my best, for the rest of Christmas vacation, to recapture the earliest days of fourteen.

Mona-Mona-Bo-Bona,
Bonano-Fano-Fo-Fona

15 "Hey, Kjersten—I can play 'The Star-Spangled Banner' in armpit farts; wanna see?"
"Antsy, you're so funny!"

There's something to be said for immaturity—acting your shoe size instead of your age, although in my case they're starting to get close. Once I gave in to it, it was fun. Dumb jokes, bathroom humor, pretending to care about stuff I gave up in middle school . . . who could have known dating an older woman could be like this?

"This is just, like, the coolest video game, Kjersten. You're driving a killer Winnebago, and everyone you run over becomes a soul trapped in your motor home. Isn't it totally great?"
"You play, Antsy. I'll just watch."

I was Kjersten's escape. It made her feel good, and that made *me* feel good. I even learned to make myself get red in the face and look all embarrassed, when I actually wasn't.

"See these scabs, like, on my elbows and stuff? They're from skateboarding. I've been, y'know, like, practicing my varial kick-flip and stuff. Like."

"So the skateboard I got you is a good one?"

"It's the best!"

The problem with stunting your own growth like that, though, is that it doesn't leave you with anything lasting. It's like eating cotton candy all day, although not quite as bad on your teeth. It's also exhausting. After a day with Kjersten, I'd just want to go home and read a newspaper or something—or even bus tables at the restaurant, just to gain back some basic level of age appropriateness. Unfortunately, I was still banned from the restaurant, and I didn't know if I'd ever be allowed back.

"What's with you?" Mom asked. I had just spent an energy-intensive day with Kjersten at the arcade and was now lying lumplike on the sofa, staring at the stock-market quotes scrolling on the financial network.

"Nothing," I answered, so Christina took it upon herself to elaborate.

"His girlfriend is using him to recapture her lost youth."

This confused Mom. "What do you mean 'lost youth'? She's only sixteen!"

"You know how it is," Christina says. "Everything starts younger and younger these days."

"It's not a problem," I told her. "I know what I'm doing."

Mom shook her head. "Lost youth! What is she gonna have you do? Wear diapers?"

"Yeah, and she burps me real good, too," I said.

Mom threw her hands up as she left the room. "I didn't just hear that."

My return to school after the holidays was met with much congratulations and pats on the back from friends and kids I didn't even know. At first I thought it was kudos for being publicly seen dating Kjersten, but it was all because of the *New York Post*. Dumping water on a senator and getting front-page exposure made me a school hero, but it was not the kind of fame I wanted.

"I could say 'I knew you when,'" Howie told me, as if this would launch me into full-on celebrity status. "Have you gotten any talk-show invitations?"

For a moment I imagined myself holding a pitcher of ice water next to Clicking Raoul on a talk show, but I shook the image away before it could do any damage.

People had no idea how the ice-water incident had affected my family. How it strained my father and the restaurant. I just wanted it to go away—why couldn't anyone understand that?

I also wanted Gunnar's rally to go away. A fake rally about

fake time, when real time was ticking away. Twenty-three days until he and his family had to be out. Were they even doing anything about it?

It actually snowed on Tuesday night—the first snow of the winter, and I hoped we'd have a snow day, postponing or even canceling the rally on Wednesday night. But who was I kidding? There's got to be woolly mammoth walking down the street before the New York City schools call a snow day.

Gunnar came up to me at my locker on Wednesday morning. Considering the looming foreclosure, I decided not to take my frustration out on him—even if he was at the root of it.

"What are you going to say at the rally tonight?" he asked.

"I don't know," I told him. "What do you think I should say?"

"You're not going to ruin it, are you?"

Did he really think I would tell everyone the truth now? How could I? I was like his partner in crime now—an accomplice. The only way to make this go away was to go through with it. Who knows, maybe as wrong as it was, it was the right thing to do. Didn't some famous dead artist say that everyone gets fifteen minutes of fame? Who was I to stand in the way of Gunnar's?

"Maybe I oughta turn the whole thing into a cash collection for your mortgage," I told him. I don't know whether he thought I was serious or just being sarcastic. That's okay, because I didn't know either.

"Too late for that," he said. "Knowing my father, the money wouldn't go to the mortgage anyway."

"Do your parents know about this rally? Do they have any idea how far this Dr. G thing has gone?"

Gunnar shrugged. Clearly they had no idea. "My mom got snowed in in Stockholm. She won't be back until late tonight. And my dad . . . well, I guess he cares more about his cards than his kids."

I was really starting to understand Gunnar's phantom illness. The Ümlauts were losing everything they owned; Gunnar's father was gambling away whatever was left and had practically abandoned his wife and kids in the process. In some ways it was probably easier for Gunnar to think he was dying than have to face all that. I thought about my father and how everything had gotten so frayed between us—but as bad as things were, deep down I knew it would all eventually blow over. We would recover. But there was no promise of recovery between Gunnar and his father. They were like the Roadkyll Raccoon danglers. Rescue was a slim hope, at best.

"I'm sure your father cares about you," I told Gunnar. "He's just messed up."

"He doesn't have a right to be messed up until he takes care of the messes he's already made."

I didn't know how to answer that, so instead I answered his original question.

"I'm going to give a speech about Pulmonary Monoxic Systemia, and thank everyone for their time donations. I'm going to say decent things about you. Then I'm going to call you up to the podium."

"Me?"

"It's your life. That thermometer's measuring years for you. You're the one who has to thank people—make them feel good about what they've done."

Gunnar couldn't look at me. He looked down, tapped the edge of my locker door with his foot. Then he said, "Dr. G isn't always wrong."

"Well . . . I hope he's wrong this time, because as screwed up as this whole thing is, I don't want you to die."

The bell rang, but Gunnar didn't leave yet. He hung around for a good ten seconds, then said, "Thanks, Antsy," and hurried off to class.

The rally was at six, on account of it couldn't interfere with class instruction or sports—but since it was approved by the district superintendent, who was up-and-coming in her political career, it was taken very seriously. I was hoping that since it was in the evening, a lot of kids wouldn't show—but then the principal offered every student who came extra credit in the class of their choosing. That was almost as good as free food.

I went home at the end of the school day, figuring I'd be home just long enough to shower, and change, and pray for an asteroid to wipe out all human life before I had to give my speech. When I got out of the shower, Mom accosted me in the hallway.

"Get dressed, we're picking up Aunt Mona at the airport."

I just stood there with a towel around me and a sinkhole opening beneath my feet.

"Don't give me that look," she said. "Her flight arrives in less than an hour." I could tell Mom was already at the end of her rope, and the visit hadn't even started. "Please, Antsy, don't make this any harder than it needs to be."

"But . . . but I got something I gotta do!"

"It can wait."

I laughed nervously, imagining an auditorium full of people waiting, and waiting and waiting. The one thing worse than having to give this speech was not showing up at all.

"You don't understand . . . I'm giving a speech tonight for that friend of mine." And this next part I had to force out, because it wasn't coming by itself. "The one who's dying."

That gave her a moment's pause. "You're giving a speech?"

"Yeah. The district superintendent is going to be there and everything."

"Why is this the first we're hearing about this?"

"Well, maybe if you two weren't at the restaurant all the time, you would have heard." I didn't mean that, but I chose to play the guilt card because this was serious, and I had to use every weapon at my disposal.

"What time does it start?" she asked.

"Six."

"Well, if you're giving a speech, we'll all want to be there. We can pick up your aunt and make it back by six."

"You can't be serious! LaGuardia Airport at this time of day? In this weather? We'll be lucky if we're back for the Fourth of July!"

But Mom wasn't caving. "Don't worry—your father knows shortcuts. Now go put on that shirt Aunt Mona bought you."

At last I lost all power of speech. Of all the days to have to wear that stupid pink-and-orange shirt—was I going to have to give a speech in front of the entire student body looking like a cross between a Barbie car and a traffic cone? My mouth hung open, something sounding like Morse code came out, and Mom said:

"Just do it," and she went downstairs to give the living room a final dusting.

I stewed all the way to LaGuardia.

"Stop pouting," Mom said, as if this was a mere childish expression of disappointment.

Well, you asked for it, I told myself. *You asked for an asteroid and here it is. Planetoid Mona, impact at 4:26 P.M., Eastern Standard Time.*

As much as I hated having to give a speech, I didn't want to be a no-show for Gunnar. All could be lost today if we didn't make it back. My good standing with the principal, my self-respect—even Kjersten, who did not approve of Gunnar's rally but would approve even less of me skipping out on him. And would Mona take the fall for this? Would my parents? No! It would all be on my head.

I cursed myself for not having the guts to say no and stick by it, refusing to go.

"Why do we all have to be at the airport?" I had said just before we left the house. "If the rest of you are there, why do *I* have to go?"

"Because I'm asking you to," was my father's response.

And as unreasonable as that was, I knew I had to go. Maybe Gunnar's dad has forfeited his right to be respected—but I still had to respect my father's wishes. Even if they screwed me royally.

By the time we got to the terminal, Aunt Mona was already waiting, and even before she hugged us, the onslaught began.

"Ugh! Where were you? I've been here for ten minutes!"

"Couldn't find parking," Dad said, kissing her cheek. "Your luggage come yet?"

"You know LaGuardia. Ugh! I'll be lucky if it comes at all." She looked at me and nodded approvingly. "I see you're wearing that shirt I got you. It's European, you know. I got it especially for you—the bright colors are supposed to make you look muscular."

Out of the corner of my eye I saw Christina grin, and I sniffed loudly to remind her she stunk of Mona's perfume. I looked at my watch—Mom saw me, and tried to rush everything along. Luckily the luggage came out quickly, and we hurried to the car, with less than an hour to make it to the rally.

Air travel was not a good thing for my aunt's mood. Our car ride was a veritable feast of unpleasantness—but rather than going through everything Mona said on the car ride, I'll offer you a menu of choice selections.

Moná
An all-you-can-stomach experience.

——— APPETIZERS ———

"I see you've still got the same old car.
Do they even make this model anymore?"

"Where are you taking us? You never had a sense of direction, Joe.
Even as a boy he'd get lost on his bicycle and I'd have to find him."

"You should smile more, Angela.
Maybe then your children might."

——— WHINE LIST ———

"Ugh! I'm an icicle here—this heater gives no heat!"

"Toxic mold in your basement? Ugh!
You should have had the whole house torn down."

"Can't we stop and get something to drink?
I'm getting nauseous from the fumes. Ugh!"*

——— SOUPS AND STEWS ———

"Traffic? You don't know traffic until you've lived in Chicago.
Your traffic is nothing compared to mine."

"Stress? You don't know stress until you've run a perfume company.
Your stress is nothing compared to what I go through."

"Weather? You don't know how easy you have it!
Come to Chicago if you want to know what real weather is."

---

*(I SUGGESTED A PITCHER OF WATER, BUT MOM REACHED OVER CHRISTINA
AND SMACKED ME.)

―――――――― MAIN COURSE ――――――――
(Served scalding hot, and taken with a grain of salt)

"You're taking me to *Paris, Capisce?* for dinner?
I thought we were going to a regular restaurant."

"It's on Avenue T? Couldn't you find a better location?
Well, I suppose you'll do better in a neighborhood
with low expectations."

"Once I move to New York, I'll be able to give you pointers
on the right way to run a business."*

―――――――― LIGHTER SELECTIONS ――――――――
for the calorie-conscious

"Angela, dear—I'll order Nutri-plan diet meals for you.
You don't have to thank me, it's my treat."

"Christina, you're very attractive, for a girl of your build."

"One word, Joe: 'Liposuction.'"

―――――――― DESSERT ――――――――

"What's this about stopping at a school?"

―――――――――――――――――――――――――――――――――――――――

*(AT THIS POINT DAD REACHED TO THE DASHBOARD, AND FOR THE BRIEFEST INSANE MOMENT, I THOUGHT HE MIGHT BE REACHING FOR AN EJECTION BUTTON THAT WOULD SEND AUNT MONA FLYING THROUGH THE ROOF—BUT HE WAS JUST TURNING ON THE RADIO.)

"How long is this going to take?"

"I haven't eaten all day!"

"Can I just wait in the car?"

"On second thought, no. In this neighborhood I'll probably get mugged."

We walked into the rally five minutes late, to find an auditorium packed, standing room only. My parents were completely bewildered. They knew I'd been doing "something" for Gunnar, but I don't think they had any idea what it was, or how big it had become. They had never even seen my time contracts.

"Some turnout," said Dad.

"And on a school night," said Mom.

"This is how flu epidemics start," said Mona, zeroing in on one kid with a hacking cough.

"What's that up onstage?" my mom asked, pointing at the big cardboard thermometer.

"It's measuring all the time I collected for Gunnar."

"Oh," she said, with no idea what I was talking about. It was actually kind of nice to see my parents starstruck by something I had done—even if it was all a sham.

I had my speech in my pocket, and as nervous as I was to get up in front of all these people, I was relieved to actually be there. This wouldn't be so bad. It would be over quick, then we could get off to dinner and face a new menu of perspiration-inducing gripes from our own "relative humidity."

But it didn't happen that way. Not by a long shot. That night will be branded in my mind forever, because it was, without exaggeration, the worst night of my life.

The Day That Forever Will Be
Known as "Black Wednesday"

16 The freezing rain had turned to sleet. It pelted the long windows of the auditorium with a clattering hiss like radio static. There were no seats for us—in fact, there were no seats for about a dozen people standing in the back, and even more were still filing in.

"This is very impressive," Mom said.

"Ugh," said Mona. "What is this, Ecuador? Do we need all this heat?"

She was right about that. Even though it was freezing outside, the auditorium was stifling hot. My father had taken off his coat, but there was nowhere to put it. He ended up holding his own and Mona's, which was made of so many small animals, my father looked like a fur trader. Mom took out a tissue and blotted his forehead since his hands were too full to do it himself.

"Antsy! Where have you been?" It was Neena Wexler, Freshman Class President.

"Airport."

Neena gave a nod of hello to my family. Mona fanned herself in response to point out the heat issue.

"Sorry it's so hot," Neena said, "but it's actually on purpose. We have a whole thermometer motif."

"Just remember to enunciate," Aunt Mona advised me. "I'm sure you'll do fine even with that speech impediment." She was referring to my apparent inability to pronounce her name "Moná."

I looked to Dad to make sure he was okay with all of this. Now that he had gotten over his initial bewilderment, he just looked tired and worried.

"Don't mind your father," Mom said. "He's just concerned because he left Barry in charge of the restaurant tonight." Barry is his assistant manager, who gets overwhelmed if there's too many salad orders.

With the clock ticking, Neena grabbed my wrist and dragged me toward the stage.

"We're all proud of you," Mom called after me.

Neena had led the entire thermometer campaign, and had done it with the brutal resolve of a wartime general. She did everything short of wrestling the entire time-shaving industry out of my hands in her attempt to make it a student-government operation. I wish I could have just left it in her hands and walked away, but I was as much a poster child for this Event as Gunnar—and make no mistake about it, this was an Event, with a capital *E*.

There were several chairs onstage, next to the thermometer. Balloons were strung to everything onstage, enough maybe to lift someone else up to the Empire State Building if you bunched them all up together. Gunnar was in one chair, and seemed to be enjoying this much more than I wanted him to. Principal Sinclair sat in another chair, and the third one was waiting for me. Some seats in the front row of the auditorium were taped off, intended for Gunnar's family, but Kjersten was the only one there. She smiled at me and I gave her a little wave. I could tell she wanted this over just as much as I did—it was good to know I wasn't the only one.

Neena whisked me past the superintendent of schools and her entourage. She shook my hand, and before I could say anything, Neena pulled me up onstage and sat me down in my preassigned seat, under bright lights that made it all the more hot.

"Interesting shirt," Gunnar said.

"'*True color coordination lies within*,'" I told him. "Tommy Freakin' Hilfiger." If Gunnar could do it, then so could I.

"Hey, Antsy," someone in the audience shouted. "You gonna baptize anyone today?"

People laughed. I couldn't find the heckler in the audience, but I did find my father, who showed no sign of amusement.

Neena approached the podium, tapped the microphone to make sure it was on, and began. "Welcome to our rally in support of our classmate and friend Gunnar Ümlaut." Cheers and whoops from the crowd. Gunnar waved; for the first time since I knew him, he seemed blissfully happy. He was milking it for all it was worth.

"You're not the homecoming king," I whispered to him. "Stop waving already."

He spoke back to me through a gritted-teeth smile, like a ventriloquist. "It would be suspicious to ignore the cheers."

Neena continued. "It's your heartfelt donations that have made this evening possible."

I pulled my speech out of my pocket, ready to give it, but Gunnar handed me a program, printed up special for the rally. "I'd put that speech away for a while if I were you," he said.

Neena, who I'm sure will grow up to plan weddings and Super Bowl halftime shows, had a whole evening of Gunnar-themed activities lined up. The program was four pages long, and "Speech by Anthony Bonano" was toward the bottom of page four. I groaned, and Neena said:

"Let's all rise for the national anthem, as performed by our jazz choir."

The curtain opened behind us to reveal the entire jazz choir wearing TIME WARRIOR T-shirts, like everyone else onstage except me and Gunnar. They delivered a painfully drawn-out rendition of "The Star-Spangled Banner," then someone in the audience yelled, "Play ball!" and the choir disappeared behind the closing curtain.

Next came an address from the principal. He talked up the school, the faculty, he kissed up to the superintendent, and then he went right into infomercial mode. "Let me just tell you about some of the many student organizations, clubs, and activities we have on our exceptional campus . . ."

Way in the back I could see Aunt Mona's lips moving and my dad nodding, taking in whatever she was spouting. I took a deep shuddering breath, and fiddled with my speech until it was all crumpled.

"I'm sorry you have to go through this," Gunnar said, "but look at how happy everyone is. They all feel like they've done a good deed just by being here."

"It doesn't get you off the hook," I reminded him.

Principal Sinclair sat down, and Neena took the podium again. "And now we're happy to present a short film made by our very own Ira Goldfarb."

"Ira?" I said aloud. I found him in the second row. He gave me a thumbs-up. I had no idea he was involved with this at all.

The auditorium darkened, and on the TVs in the corner we viewed a ten-minute documentary featuring interviews with students and teachers, candid moments of Gunnar that he didn't even know about, and a painfully detailed, animated description of Pulmonary Monoxic Systemia that would make most of my speech seem redundant. The whole thing was done to songs like "Wind Beneath my Wings" and "We Are the Champions." The fact that Ira had half the audience in tears after the last slow-motion sequence made me more impressed, and more annoyed, by his filmmaking skills than ever before. Gunnar was still grinning like an idiot, but I could tell he was getting embarrassed. This was too much attention, even for him.

When it was over, the lights came up, and Neena rose to the podium once more. "Wasn't that wonderful?" she asked, not expecting a response, although some bozo yelled that he wet his pants. "But before we go on," said Neena, "let's have a look at the thermometer." She pulled the microphone from its holder and crossed to the thermometer, which stood taller than she did. "As you can see our goal is fifty years. Right now, we only have forty-seven years and five months, but tonight we're going to reach our goal!"

The audience applauded with questionable enthusiasm.

"Who out there would like to help us reach our goal for Gunnar?"

She waited. And she waited. And she waited some more.

Gunnar and I looked at each other, starting to get uncomfortable. Neena, perfectionist that she is, was not willing to leave it at forty-seven years, five months. The thermometer had to be complete. There was a red Sharpie standing by for that very purpose, and no one—*no one*—was going anywhere until Gunnar had a full fifty years.

"Isn't there anyone out there willing to give the tiniest amount of goodwill to Gunnar?" urged Neena.

Principal Sinclair took to the microphone. "Come on, people! I know for a fact that our students here are more generous than this!" And that clinched it—because now filling up the thermometer was far less entertaining than making us all sit up there looking foolish.

Finally Wailing Woody rose from his seat and came down the aisle, high-fiving everyone as he passed. As he came up to the stage he raised his hands as if to quiet nonexistent applause. He gave a month, and was quickly followed by the superintendent and her entourage. The applause was getting weaker and less enthusiastic with each signature.

"Okay," said Neena. "That makes forty-eight years, even. Who's next?"

I leaned over to her. "Neena," I whispered, "this isn't a telethon, we don't have to reach the goal."

"Yes! We! Do!" she snapped back in the harshest whisper I've ever heard. I looked to Principal Sinclair, but he was intimidated by her, too.

No one was stepping forward, and I was beginning to wonder if maybe Neena might put the school into lockdown, and we'd be there until morning. Then, from the back of the room, I heard, "Oh, for goodness' sake!" And my salvation came marching down the center aisle.

My father!

I could not have been more grateful as he made his way to the stage. After all I had put him through, here he was saving the day!

Neena reached out to shake his hand, but his expression definitely lacked the spirit Neena was looking for, and she put her hand down.

"How much do you need?" he asked, getting right to business.

"Two years," Nina answered.

"You got it. Where do I sign?"

I took a time contract and handed it to my father, showing what to fill in, and where to sign.

"Thank you, Dad," I said. "Really."

"Your aunt is driving us crazy," he told me. "It was either this or a grudge match between her and your mother." He wiped sweat from his brow, then signed the document. The principal signed as witness, and Neena snatched the paper, holding it up to the audience.

"Mr. Bonano has given us two full years! We've reached our goal!" And the crowd went wild, whooping and hollering at the prospect of moving on to page three.

Dad shook Gunnar's hand, turned to leave the stage . . . then he hesitated. He turned to me, wiping his forehead again. It was the first time that I noticed he was sweating a bit more than anyone else onstage. He looked pale, too, and it wasn't just the stage lights.

"Dad?"

He waved me off. "I'm fine."

Then he rubbed his chest, took a deep breath, and suddenly fell to one knee.

"Dad!"

I was down there with him in an instant. A volley of gasps came from the audience, blending with the clatter of sleet on the windows.

"Joe!" I hear my mother scream.

"I'm okay. It's nothing. I'm fine."

But now he went all the way down, on all fours. "I . . . I just need someone to help me up." But instead of getting up, he kept going down. In a second he had rolled over and was flat on his back, struggling to breathe.

And still my father insists that everything's okay. I want to believe him. This is not happening, I tell myself. And if I say it enough, maybe I'll believe it.

From this moment on, nothing made proper sense. Everything was random shouts and disconnected images. Time fell apart.

Mom is there holding his hand.

Mona's on the stage, clutching her coat beside her, and gets pushed out of the way by the security guard who claims to know CPR, but doesn't seem too confident.

A million cell phones dialing 911 all at once.

"I'm fine. I'm fine. Oh God."

Gunnar standing next to Kjersten standing next to me, none of us able to do a damn thing.

The guard counting, and doing chest compressions.

The whole audience standing like it's the national anthem all over again.

Dad's not talking anymore.

The squealing wheels of a gurney rolling down the aisle. How did they get here so fast? How long has he been lying on that stage?

An oxygen mask, and his fingers feel so cold, and the crowd parts before us as the wheels squeal again, and me, Mom, Christina, and Mona are carried along in the wake of the gurney toward the auditorium door, where cold air rolls in, hitting the heat and making fog that rolls like ocean surf.

And in the madness of this terrible moment, one voice in the crowd, loud and clear, pierces the panic. Once voice that says:

"My God! He gave two years, and he died!"

I turn to seek out the owner of that voice. "SHUT UP!" I scream. "SHUT UP! HE'S NOT DEAD!" If I found who said it, I'd break him up so bad he'd be joining us at the hospital, but I'm pulled along too quickly in the gurney's wake, out the door and into the wet night. He's not dead. He's not. Even as they load him into the ambulance, they're talking to him, and he's nodding. Weakly, but he's nodding.

We pile into our car to follow, leaving Gunnar, and Kjersten, and the thermometer and the crowd. Now there's nothing but the sleet, and the cold, and the wail and flashing lights of the ambulance as we break every traffic law and run every red light to keep up with it, because we don't know which hospital they're taking him to, so we can't lose the ambulance. We can't. We can't.

My Head Explodes Like Mount St. Helens, and I'll Probably Be Picking Up the Pieces for Years

17 Our lives get spent worrying about such pointless, stupid things. Does this girl like me? Does this boy know I exist? Did I get an A, B, or C? And will everyone laugh when they see my ugly shirt? It's amazing how quickly—how, in the smallest moment of time, all of that can implode into nothing, when the universe suddenly opens up, revealing itself with all these impossible depths and dizzying heights. You're swept up into it, and as you look down, the perspective is terrifying. People look like ants from so far away.

I understand hell now, and you don't have to leave this world to get there. You can get there just fine sitting in a hospital waiting room.

Coney Island Hospital's emergency room didn't seem to have much to do with health. It seemed more like this sickly mix of bad luck, bad timing, and even worse news. My father got rushed in right away, and the rest of us were left to wait in the reception area, where people who weren't immediately dying waited for service like it was a deli counter.

"Did they have to bring him here?" says Aunt Mona. "What's wrong with Kings County, or Maimonides?"

There were a lot of people with bloody clothes, poorly bandaged wounds, and bloated, feverish faces—all hanging their hopes on a single overtired receptionist who was, in theory, calling names, although it was more than half an hour until I heard her call a single one. I tried to read a magazine, but couldn't focus. Christina played halfheartedly with a battered old Boggle game she got from a toy chest that smelled of small children. Mom seemed to be studying the pattern of the carpet.

"Why aren't they telling us anything?" says Aunt Mona. "I don't like how they run this hospital."

There was a huge fish tank filled with fake coral rocks and a plastic diver all covered with green tank scum. There seemed to be only three fish in the giant tank, and I'm thinking, *If this place can't take care of their fish, what does it say about patient care?*

"I don't know what this stain on this seat is," says Aunt Mona, "but I'm going to sit over there."

My phone rang. I didn't recognize the number, so I didn't pick up. But then it had been ringing a lot, and I hadn't picked up for anybody. Thinking of the phone reminded me of something.

"You gotta call Frankie," I told Mom.

Mom shook her head. "Not yet."

"You gotta call Frankie!" I told her more forcefully.

"If I do, he'll come driving all the way from Binghamton in

the middle of the night in this weather at a hundred miles an hour! No thank you, I don't need two in the hospital! We'll call your brother in the morning."

I was about to protest—but then I got it. Even though I couldn't see the look in her eyes, I got it. *You gather the whole family at a deathbed.* So as long as Frankie's not here, it's not a deathbed, is it? It's the same reason she hadn't asked to talk to a priest.

My phone rang again, and I finally turned it off. Did people think I would actually answer it? As if their need to know was more important than my need not to talk about it.

An hour later a doctor came out and asked for Mrs. Benini. I took no notice until Mom says, "Do you mean Bonano?"

The doctor looked at his chart and corrected himself. "Yes—Bonano."

Suddenly I think the heart attack might have spread to me. We all stand up.

"Mrs. Bonano," the doctor said, "your husband has an acute blockage of the—"

But that's all I hear, because I get stuck on one word.

Has.

Present tense! "Has" means "is," not "was." It means my father's alive. Never have I appreciated tense so completely. I swore I'll never take tense for granted again.

"He's going to need emergency bypass surgery," the doctor told us. "Triple bypass, actually." The fact that they had a name for it was a good thing, I figured. If they knew what they had to do, then they could do it, but Mom covered her mouth and found a new wellspring of tears, so I knew this wasn't so good.

"It's a long operation, but your husband's a fighter," the doctor said. "I have every hope that he'll pull through." And then he added, "There's a chapel on the second floor, if you'd like some privacy." Which is not something you say to someone if you truly believe their loved one is going to pull through.

The doctor said he'd keep us posted, and disappeared through the double doors. Mom said nothing. Christina and I said nothing. But Aunt Mona said, "It's all that cholesterol in his diet. I've warned him for years. Our father, rest his soul, went the same way, but did Joe listen?"

Back in eighth grade, I had a geology unit in science. We studied volcanoes. Some erupt predictably, spewing magma, and others just explode. The rock is so hot it actually becomes gas, and the blast is more powerful than a hydrogen bomb.

That's the closest I can come to explaining what happened to me next. I could feel it coming the moment Aunt Mona opened her mouth, and I had no way to control it.

Mom saw me about to blow. She tried to grab me, but I shook her off. There was no stopping this—not by her, not by anybody.

"Shut your freaking mouth!" I screamed. Everyone in the waiting room turned to me, but I didn't care. *"Shut your freaking mouth before I shut it for you!"* Mona gaped, unable to speak as I looked her in the eye, refusing to look away. *"You sit there and complain every day of your stupid life, passing judgment on everyone, and even now you won't shut up!"*

And then I said it. I said the words that had been brewing inside since the moment my father went down on that stage.

"It should have been you."

She looked at me like I had plunged a dagger through her heart.

"Anthony!" my mother said, losing all her wind with that single word.

I kept Mona locked in my gaze, feeling as if my eyes could just burn her away. *"It should be you in that operating room. I wish it was you dying instead of him."*

So now it was out. I meant it, she knew I meant it—everyone in the waiting room knew.

And from somewhere beside me, I heard Christina, in a tiny voice say, "So do I . . ."

Suddenly it felt like there was no air in that room, and the walls had closed in. I had to escape. I don't even remember leaving. The next thing I knew I was in the parking garage, searching for our car, and I found it. I didn't have the keys, but Mom, in her panic, had forgotten to lock it. Good thing, too, because I was fully prepared to break a window. I almost wanted to.

I sat in the car that smelled so strongly of Aunt Mona's perfume, and I pounded the dashboard. Mona was the one with all the anxiety. She was a human propeller churning up stress until everyone was drowning in it. Why couldn't it have been her? Why?

I was starting to cool down by the time my mom came, and sat in the car beside me.

"No lectures!" I yelled, even before she opened her mouth.

"No lectures," she agreed quietly.

We sat there for a while in silence, and when she finally did speak, she said, "Aunt Mona decided it was best if she took a hotel room across the street from the hospital. That way she can be close." Which meant she wouldn't be staying with us anymore. I wondered if I'd ever see her again. I wondered if I cared.

"Good," I said. I might have cooled down, but it didn't change what I said, or the fact that I meant it. But then my mother said something I didn't see coming.

"Anthony . . . don't you realize I was thinking the same thing?"

I looked to her, not sure that I had heard her right. "What?"

"From the moment I knew your father was having a heart attack, I had to fight to keep it out of my mind. *'It should have been her, not Joe—it should have been her . . .'*" Mom closed her eyes, and I could see her trying to force the worst of those god-awful feelings away. "But honey, there are some things that must never be said out loud."

Knowing she was right just made me angrier. I gritted my teeth so hard I thought I might break them—and then what? We'd have dental bills on top of bypass.

"I'm not sorry."

Mom patted my arm. "That's okay," she said. "Someday you will be, and you can deal with it then."

Somewhere in the garage a car alarm went off, echoing all around.

"No word from the doctor?" I asked.

"Not yet. But that's good."

I knew what she meant. It was a four-, maybe five-hour oper-ation. There's only one reason it would end early.

"I'd better get back," Mom said. "Come when you're ready. We'll be in the chapel." And she left.

My anger at the unfairness of it all still raged inside, but some of that anger was bouncing off of Mona and sticking to me. Wasn't I the one who dumped that pitcher of water on Boswell, making life that much harder on my father? Wasn't I always talking back, creating problems, making things harder at home? Could I have been the one who pushed him one step too far?

And then I got to thinking about the time contracts, and how I, in a way, had been tempting fate—playing God. Was this my punishment? Was this, as they say, the wage of my sin?

My brain had already turned to cottage cheese, and now it was going funnier still. You can call it another volcanic burst, you can call it temporary insanity, you can call it whatever you like. All I know is that in my current dairy-brained state, the letters in my own mental Boggle game suddenly came together and started talking in tongues.

Fact: My father's heart attack happened within moments of him signing a contract for two years of his life.

Fact: It was my fault the contract even existed.

Fact: There was a fat black binder filled with almost fifty years sitting in Gunnar Ümlaut's bedroom.

. . . but I could get those years back.

Maybe if I got all those pages and brought them to my father—or better yet, brought them to the chapel and laid them down on the altar . . . Did a hospital chapel have an altar? If not, I would make one. I'd take a table, and sprinkle it with holy water. I'd renounce what I had done—truly renounce it, and those pages would be my bargain with God. Then, once that bargain had been struck, the morning would come, the operation would be a success, and I would still have a father.

This wasn't just an answer, it felt like a vision! I could almost hear the gospel choir singing the hallelujahs.

I left the car, my breath coming in fast puffs of steam in the midnight cold, and took to the street, searching for the nearest subway station.

Go Ahead . . . Tenderize My Meat.

18 There were things I didn't know, which I didn't find out until much later—like what happened in the auditorium after my father was rushed out.

My God—he gave two years of his life and he died!

It hadn't occurred to me that others had heard that—and even though news of my father's death had been greatly exaggerated, it didn't matter. What mattered was the possibility that he'd die. Just like my eruption at Aunt Mona, it was something everyone was thinking, but it was too dangerous to say aloud.

In the awkward, uneasy moments after we had left, Principal Sinclair tried to get things back on track—the show must go on, and all. It was no use. The crowd was murmuring up a cloud of worry—not about my father, but about themselves. Then someone yelled, "Hey, I want my month back," and all eyes turned to Gunnar.

In less than a minute, people were asking him, tugging at him, grabbing at him, demanding their time back—and when he didn't give it back right then and there, things started to get ugly. People were yelling, pushing one another, and then kids who didn't even care took this as their cue to make further mischief, by fighting, throwing stuff, and creating a general atmosphere of havoc. Mob mentality took over.

Gunnar and Kjersten escaped through a back door, along with the superintendent, leaving poor Mr. Sinclair and a skeletal faculty desperately struggling to bring back sanity, like that was gonna happen. In the end, Wendell Tiggor led about twenty semihardened criminals and delinquent wannabes on a rampage through the school. The rest was history.

But I didn't know any of this when I arrived at Gunnar and Kjersten's house at twelve-thirty in the morning.

I rang the bell and knocked, rang and knocked, over and over until Mrs. Ümlaut came to the door in a bathrobe. There was luggage just inside the door, and I knew she must have arrived home that evening. I didn't bother with pleasantries, I pushed right past her and bounded up the stairs.

"What are you doing? What do you want?" she wailed, but I really didn't have time for explanations.

Gunnar's door was closed, but not locked. The one thing I had going for me tonight was unlocked doors. I found a light switch, flicked it on, and Gunnar sat up in bed, blinking, not entirely conscious yet.

"Where is it?" I demanded.

"Antsy? Wh-what's going on?"

"The notebook. Where is it? Answer me!"

It took him a moment to process the question, then he glanced over at his desk. "It's there, but—"

That's all I needed to know. I grabbed the notebook—and noticed right away that it felt way too light. I opened it up and saw that it was empty. The pages were all gone.

"Where's all the time? I have to have that time!"

"You can't!" Gunnar said.

Wrong answer! I pulled him out of bed so sharply, I heard his T-shirt tear. "You're giving them to me, and you're giving them to me now!" I never muscled other kids to get what I want, but right now I was willing to use every muscle in my body to get this.

Behind me I heard Kjersten call my name, I heard their mother scream, and that pushed me all the more to push him. I slammed Gunnar hard against the wall. "Give them to me!"

Then something hit me. Mrs. Ümlaut had attacked me. She was armed, and swinging, wailing as she did. I felt the weapon connect with my back, the blow softened slightly by my jacket, but still it hurt. She swung it again, and this time I saw what it was. It was a meat tenderizer. A stainless-steel, square little mallet. She swung the kitchen utensil like the hammer of Thor and it connected with my shoulder right through my coat.

"Ow!"

"You stop this!" she screamed. "You stop this now!"

But I didn't stop. I didn't stop until Kjersten entered the battle, and with a single blow that bore the force of the dozen or so other Norse gods, her fist connected with my face and I went down.

You don't know this kind of pain—and if you do, I'm sorry.

Had it been my nose, she would have broken it. Had it been my chin, my jaw would have to be wired together for months. But it was my eye.

All those muscles that were, just an instant ago, ready to tear Gunnar limb from limb suddenly decided it was time to call it a night, and they all went limp. I didn't quite pass out, but I did find myself on the ground, with just enough strength to bring my hands to my eye, and cry out in pain.

My left eye was swollen shut in seconds, and in the kind of humiliation beyond which there is only darkness, I allowed Kjersten to guide me downstairs and into the kitchen. I had just been beaten to a pulp by my girlfriend in a single blow. Social lives did not get any bleaker than this.

"I had to do it," she said as she prepared a bag of ice for me. "If I didn't, my mother would have taken that meat tenderizer to your head, and knocked you silly."

"Silly works," I mumbled. "Better than where I was."

She seemed to understand, even without me telling her— after all, she was right there in the front row when my dad had the heart attack. I told her where things stood with my father, and she went out into the living room, explaining everything to her mother. She spoke in Swedish, which, I guess was the language of love in this family. I could see Mrs. Ümlaut glance at me as they spoke. At first she looked highly suspicious, but her distrust eventually faded, and her motherly instincts returned.

Gunnar joined me in the kitchen. It kind of surprised me on account of we now had a perp/victim relationship. He seemed unfazed by my unprovoked attack. Maybe because there were plenty of other things to faze him.

"I don't think we're going to be a National Blue Ribbon school," he said, and he explained to me the madness that ensued after my family and I had left the rally.

"I couldn't give anyone back their months," he said. "You can't have them either. Because last week my dad found them, and burned them all in the fireplace."

And there they went, all my hopes of redemption up in smoke. Without those time contracts, I could not undo what I had done. But I had already regained enough of my senses to realize getting those pages would not help my father.

Gunnar went on to tell me how his dad had officially left the minute his mom came home.

"They're splitting up," he told me.

I almost started to say how that wasn't such a big deal, considering—but realized that I would sound just like Aunt Mona. *Trauma? You don't know from trauma until your father's had a heart attack. And they're much worse in Chicago.*

I wouldn't invalidate his pain. Every problem is massive until something more massive comes along.

In a few moments Mrs. Ümlaut came in with Kjersten. Mercifully she did not have the meat tenderizer. Mrs. Ümlaut sat beside me, far more sympathetic than when I pushed through the front door.

"Your father?" she asked.

"They're still working on him," I said. "At least they were when I left."

She nodded. Then she took my both my hands in hers, looked into my one useful eye, and then Mrs. Ümlaut said something to me that I know I will remember for the rest of my life.

"Either he will live, or he will die."

That was it. That was all. Yet suddenly everything came into clear focus. *Either he will live, or he will die.* Simple as that. All the drama, all the craziness, all the panic, didn't mean a thing. This was a gamble—a roll of the dice. I don't know why, but I took comfort from that. There were, after all, only two outcomes. I could not predict them, I could not control them. It was not in my hands. I had been afraid to say the word "die," but now that it had been said, and with such strength and compassion, it held no power over me.

For the first time all night, I found myself crying like there was no tomorrow—although I knew there would be a tomorrow. It might not be the tomorrow I wanted, but it would still be there.

I could feel Kjersten's hand on my shoulder, and I let comfort come from all sides. Then, when my tears had gone dry, Mrs. Ümlaut said, "Come, I'll take you to the hospital."

When I got to the hospital, there were more familiar faces in the waiting area. Relatives we didn't get to see this holiday season, Barry from the restaurant, a couple of family friends—and in the middle of it all were Lexie and her grandfather. I went straight to Lexie. Moxie got up when he saw me, and so Lexie knew, even before someone called my name, that I was there.

"We came as soon as we heard," she said. "Where have you been?"

"Long story. Is there any news?"

"Not yet."

I looked around. Mona had come back, and Christina was asleep in her arms. I wondered if they had made up. Mona didn't look at me.

Crawley, who never came out of his apartment unless he was kidnapped or pried out with a crowbar, came up to me. "All expenses shall be covered," he said. "Either way."

For a second I felt like getting angry at that, but I had had enough anger for one evening. "That's okay," I told him. "We don't want your money."

"But you'll take it," he said, and then added with more emotion than I'd ever seen in him before, "because that's what I have to give."

I nodded a quiet acceptance.

"Your mother's up in the chapel," Lexie said.

I gave a quick greeting to relatives and friends, then went to find her.

The place wasn't much of a chapel—there were only four rows, and the pews seemed too comfortable to be effective. There was a small stained-glass panel, backlit with fluorescent lights. There was no cross on account of it was a spiritual multipurpose room, that had to be used by people of all religious symbols. The chapel's best feature was a huge bookshelf stocked with Bibles and holy books of all shapes and sizes, so nobody got left out. Old Testament, New Testament, red testament, blue testament. This one has a little star—see how many faiths there are. (This is the moment I realized how exhausted I really was.)

Mom was alone in the room, kneeling in the second row. It was so like her to take the second row even when she was alone in the room.

"Did you fall asleep in the car?" Mom asked, without turning around to see me.

"How did you know it was me?"

"I can always tell when you need a shower," she told me. Between her and Lexie, who needed sight? At least if she didn't look at me too closely, she wouldn't see my swollen eye.

"Come pray with me, Anthony."

And so I did. I knelt beside her, joining her—and as I did, maybe for the first time in my life, I understood it. Not so much the words as the whole idea of prayer itself.

I'll never really know if prayer changes the outcome of things. Lots of people believe it does. I know I'd like to believe it, but there's no guarantee. Some people pray and their prayers are rewarded—they walk away convinced that their prayers were answered. Others pray and they get refused. Sometimes they lose their faith, all because they lost the roll of the dice.

That night, as I prayed, I wasn't praying for my own wants and needs. I prayed for my father, and for my mother, I prayed for my whole family. Not because I was *supposed* to—not because I was afraid of what would happen if I didn't. I was doing it because I truly wanted to do it with all my heart, and believe it or not, for the first time ever, I didn't want it to end.

That's when I realized—

—and excuse me for having a whole immaculate Sunday-school moment here, but I gotta milk it since they don't come that often—

—that's when I realized that prayer isn't for God. After all, He doesn't need it. He's out there, or in there, or sitting up there in His firmament, whatever that is, all-knowing and all-powerful, right? He doesn't need us repeating words week after week in His face. If He's there, sure, I'll bet He's listening, but it doesn't *change* Him, one way or the other.

Instead, *we're* the ones who are changed by it.

I don't know whether that's true, or whether I was just delirious from lack of sleep . . . but if it *is* true, what an amazing gift that is!

I let my mother decide when it was time to stop. Like I said, I could have just gone on and on. I think she knew that. I think she liked that. Then I think she started to worry that I might become a priest. This wasn't a worry of mine.

It was still the middle of the night. Three-thirty, and no word. Mom looked at me, and seemed to notice my swollen face for the first time, but chose not to ask. Instead she said, "I think you were right. Maybe I should call Frankie now."

She took out her phone and called. When it connected, the sheer look of horror on my mother's face even before she said a word got me scared, too.

"What? What is it?"

But in a moment her terror resolved into something else I couldn't quite read. "Here," she said. "Listen to the message."

I took the phone just as the message started to repeat.

"Hello. You've reached the Kings County Morgue. Our offices are closed now, but if this is a morgue-related emergency, please

dial zero. Otherwise please call back during normal business hours."

I looked at her, gaping and shaking my head. This was my doing. Just like I said, I had programmed the morgue into her speed dial as a joke, and I must have programmed it over Frankie's number. What stinking, lousy timing.

"I'm sorry," I said. "I'm so, so, sorry."

My eyes started to well up, because right here, right now, it almost seemed like a bad omen, and she was getting all choked up, too. She turned away. Then I heard her give a little hiccup, and then another, and when she turned back, I could see that in the middle of tears, she had started laughing.

"You rotten, rotten kid."

And then I was laughing, too. I put my arms around her and held her, and both of us stood there laughing, and crying, laughing and crying like a couple of nutjobs, until the doctor came in, and cleared his throat to get our attention. Maybe he understood what we were feeling, maybe he didn't. Maybe he'd seen everything. He started to speak before we had the chance to brace ourselves.

"He made it through the operation," he said, "but the next twenty-four hours are crucial."

We relaxed just the slightest bit, and Mom finally got to call Frankie instead of the morgue.

I Love You, You're an Idiot,
Now Let's All Go Home

19 My father almost died again the next day, but he didn't. Instead he started to get better. By Friday, they moved him out of intensive care, and by Saturday, he was bored. He tried to squeeze news out of my mom about the restaurant, but all she would say was, "It's there," and she forbade anyone else to talk about it, for fear that talking business would send my father back into cardiac arrest.

With my dad on the mend, and more than enough people doting on him, my thoughts drifted to Kjersten and Gunnar. I went to visit on Sunday morning, to see how they were handling their own hardships, and give whatever support I could. The Christmas wreath was gone from their door, and the foreclosure notice glared out for the whole world to see.

"Good riddance," I heard one beer-bellied neighbor say to another as I walked down the block toward their house. "After what they did to our yards, let 'em go back where they came from. Freakin' foreigners."

I turned to the man. "No, actually *I* was the one who did that to your yards, and I ain't going nowhere. You gonna do something about it?"

He puffed on a cigarette. "Why don't you just move along," he said from behind the safety of his little waist-high wrought-iron fence.

"Lucky you got that fence between us," I said. "Otherwise I might have to go samurai on your ass." I have to say there's nothing more satisfying than lip delivered to those who deserve it.

Mrs. Ümlaut answered the door, and pulled me in like she was pulling me out of a blizzard instead of a clear winter day. She barely allowed Kjersten to hug me before she dragged me into the kitchen, practically buried me in French toast, and had me tell her all about my dad's condition. Now that I had fought various members of the Ümlaut household and had been struck repeatedly by a blunt object, I guess that made me like family.

I went upstairs to find Gunnar in his room, watching a black-and-white foreign film called *The Seventh Seal.*

"It's by Ingmar Bergman, patron saint of all things Swedish," he said. "It's about a chess game with death."

"Of course it is," I said. "What else would you be watching?" I sat down at his desk chair. There was dust on his desk, as if he hadn't done homework for weeks.

"What's that thing the Grim Reaper holds, anyway?" I asked.

"It's called a scythe," Gunnar said. "It's what people used to use to harvest grain."

"So does modern death drive a combine?"

Gunnar chuckled, but only slightly.

We watched the film for a few minutes. It was a scene where the main character was looking out of a high window, supposedly facing the horizon of his own mortality, and it got me thinking about the guy who fell from the Roadkyll Raccoon balloon on Thanksgiving. I wondered if he, like the guy in the film, saw the Grim Reaper waiting for him.

No one likes the Grim Reaper. He's like that tax auditor who came to our house a couple of years ago. He's just doing his job, but everyone hates his guts on principle. If there really is such a guy and he comes for me someday, I promised myself I'd offer him cookies and milk, like little kids do for Santa Claus. Then maybe at least he'll put in a good word for me. Bribing Death never hurts.

"It's good that you're reconnecting with your roots," I told him. "I should watch more Italian films."

He turned off the TV. "I don't need to watch this," he said. "I know the ending. Death wins."

I shrugged. "Doesn't mean you gotta go carving tombstones."

Gunnar tossed the remote on his desk. "I'm done with that." He flexed his fingers. "I think maybe it gave me carpal tunnel."

He looked at his hand for a while, and although his gaze never left his fingers, I know his thoughts went far away.

"My father's at the casino again," Gunnar said. "He hasn't found a place to live yet, so I guess that's where he's staying until he does. Maybe he'll just set up a cot underneath one of the roulette wheels. I really don't care."

That, I knew, was a lie. Keep in mind that I had almost lost my father a few days before, so I knew what Gunnar was going through. It was in a different way, but the concept was basically the same. Reapers come in all shapes and sizes. And they don't always clear-cut the field with their scythes—sometimes they just leave crop circles.

I really don't care, Gunnar had said—and all at once I realized that Gunnar was finally, *finally* in denial. For him this was the best thing that could happen, and it gave me an idea.

"I know they're taking away your house," I said to him, "but do you think you guys can squeeze out enough money to fill your mom's car with gas?"

Even if the answer was no, I knew that I had enough money if they didn't.

When someone's addicted, they have these things called interventions. I know about them because my parents had to intervene for one of my dad's high school buddies who got addicted to some designer drug. Like drugs ain't bad enough, they got designers involved now. Basically everyone the guy knew sat him down in a room, told him they loved him and that he was a freakin' moron. Love and humiliation—it's a powerful combination—and it probably saved his life.

That's what I thought we'd have with Mr. Ümlaut—a feel-good, huggy-feely intervention. But it didn't quite turn out that way.

The Anawana Tribal Hotel and Casino was located deep in the Catskill Mountains, on the grounds of an old summer camp, proving that times changed. Old crumbling cabins, yellow and brown, could still be seen from the parking structure. The place boasted a riverboat that, for a few dollars more, would tool around Anawana Lake while you gambled.

The hotel's main casino was patrolled by security, but I guess Kjersten, Gunnar, and I looked old enough to pass for gambling age—or at least old enough to be ignored for a while, because they didn't stop us from going into the casino. Kjersten was quiet, steeling herself for the ambush, which is pretty much what this would be.

"Do you really think this will make a difference?" she asked me.

I had no idea, but the fact that she asked at all meant that she still had hope. She held my hand firmly, and it occurred to me that I was no longer her gateway to a younger, simpler time. In spite of our age difference, she'd never see me as "younger" again. And yet still, she was holding my hand.

We found Mr. Ümlaut playing craps. Even before he saw us, I could tell by the look on his face, and the circles under his eyes, that this was not going to be a heartwarming Hallmark moment.

He was throwing the dice, and apparently doing well. Adrenaline was high among the gamblers at the table around him.

"Dad?" said Gunnar. He had to say it again to get his attention. "Dad?"

With the dice still in his fist, he saw us, and it was like he was coming out of a dream. "Gunnar? Kjersten?" Then he saw me, and glared at me like their presence here was all my fault, which it was.

"Sir," said the craps guy, quickly sizing up the situation, "your children can't be here."

"I know." Mr. Ümlaut threw the dice anyway. I don't know much about craps, but apparently eleven was good. The other gamblers roared.

"You shouldn't be here," Mr. Ümlaut said to us. "Your mother isn't here, is she?"

"Just us, Daddy," said Kjersten gently.

"You should go home."

The craps guy handed him the dice, but was reluctant about it. Mr. Ümlaut shook the dice in his hand while the others standing around the table waited anxiously. Realizing we weren't going to simply disappear, Mr. Ümlaut said, "Go wait for me in the lobby." Then he hurled the dice again. Nine. This time only a few of the gamblers were happy.

"Sir, I'm afraid I must insist," the craps guy said, and pointed to us.

In turn, Mr. Ümlaut pointed to the lobby. "You heard the croupier!" Which sounded a whole lot classier than "craps guy." It makes you wonder why they haven't come up with a better name for craps. Croups, maybe.

By now the suit who managed the whole bank of craps tables came over. This guy's title I knew. He was the pit boss. The croupier's croupier. "Is there a problem here?" the pit boss asked.

"No," said Mr. Ümlaut. Then he whispered to Gunnar and Kjersten, "Leave the casino before you create a scene." Kjersten quietly stood her ground, but Gunnar had enough lip for both of them.

"A scene," said Gunnar. "Right." He nodded and backed away. I thought we were going to wait in the lobby, but then

Gunnar turned around in the middle of the aisle. For a second I thought he might say something meaningful and thought provoking—like maybe a really well-chosen fake quote. But no. Gunnar decided it was time to sing. This wasn't a quiet kind of singing either. He belted out at the top of his voice, and the sounds that came out of his mouth were like no words I'd ever heard.

"*Du gamla, Du fria, Du fjällhöga nord . . .*"

As far as interventions go, this was taking on a whole personality of its own.

"It's the Swedish national anthem," Kjersten explained to me.

"*Du tysta, Du glädjerika sköna!*"

Mr. Ümlaut just stared at him with the kind of shock and embarrassment that can only come from a parent.

"*Jag hälsar Dig, vänaste land uppå jord.*"

Kjersten joined in, and now it was a duet. Since I didn't know the Swedish national anthem, I improvised and began to sing the most Swedish thing I knew. I began to sing a song by that Swedish seventies group, Abba.

So now the croupier looks at the pit boss, the pit boss signals the manager, and the manager comes running.

"*Din sol, Din himmel, Dina ängder gröna.*"

All gambling in the casino grinds to a screeching halt as we perform.

"*You can dance! You can jive! Having the time of your life!*" I sing at the manager, who's much less entertained than I believe he should be.

Kjersten and Gunnar complete their anthem, and although I've still got a couple of verses of "Dancing Queen" left, I figure it's wise to wrap it up early. Some of the gamblers applaud, and not knowing what else to do, we all take fancy bows, and the manager turns to Mr. Ümlaut and says, "I think you should leave now."

Mr. Ümlaut did not look happy as we crossed the casino toward the lobby. Gunnar, on the other hand, looked downright triumphant at his little victory. Even more triumphant than he did on the night of the rally. It was Kjersten who seemed worried, because she knew as well as I did that this was just one battle in a much bigger war. The security guard escorting us must have resented that look on Gunnar's face, because he was rough with him, and got rougher when Gunnar tried to pull out of his grasp.

"Are you gonna let this rent-a-cop beat me up?"

Mr. Ümlaut didn't look at him. He didn't say a word until we were off the casino floor, and the security guard returned to his duties, satisfied that we were no longer a threat.

"Proud of yourself, Gunnar?"

"Are you?" Gunnar answered, with such righteous authority that his father couldn't look him in the eye.

"There are things you don't understand."

"I understand a lot more than you think."

Rather than letting the two of them bicker, Kjersten cut it off. "Daddy," she said, "we want you to come home."

He didn't answer right away. Instead he looked at them, perhaps searching for something in their faces, but you couldn't read much in those two—in that way, they took after their father.

"Didn't your mother tell you?" he said.

"What?" said Gunnar. "That you're splitting up? Of course she did."

It surprised me that he hadn't told them himself. Even if they already knew, he had a responsibility to say it in his own words.

"I will let you know where I am, once I know myself," he said. "There's nothing to worry about."

"There's a lot to worry about," Gunnar said—then Gunnar got closer to him. All this time he had maintained a distance from his father, like there was an invisible wall around him. Now Gunnar stepped inside that wall. "You're sick, Dad." He looked at the casino, all full of whirring, blaring, coin-clanging excitement, then turned back to his father. "You're very sick. And I think if you don't do something about it . . . if you don't stop gambling, somehow it's going to kill you."

But rather than taking it in, Mr. Ümlaut seemed to just pull his wall in closer, so Gunnar was on the outside again. "Is that what your mother says?"

"No," said Kjersten. "We figured it out for ourselves."

"I appreciate your concern," he said, like he was talking to strangers instead of his children. "I'll be fine."

"What about *them*?" I said. Maybe I was out of line speaking at all, but I had to say something.

Suddenly I found all his anger turned against me. "What business is this of yours? What do you know about our family? What do you know about anything?"

"Leave him alone!" shouted Kjersten. "At least he's around when we need him. At least he's there." Which I guess is the best you could say about me. "At least he's not away day after day, gambling away every penny he owns. How much money have you lost, Dad? Then the car—and now the house . . ."

"You're not understanding!" he said, loud enough to snag the attention of another family waiting to check in. They peered at us over their luggage, pretending not to. Mr. Ümlaut forced his voice down again. "The car, the house—we were losing them anyway—if not this month, then next month. A few dollars gambled makes no difference."

I think he truly believed that—and for the first time, I began to understand what Kjersten and Gunnar were up against. Mr. Ümlaut had, once upon a time, been a lawyer. That meant he could create a brilliant and convincing argument as to why the hours, days, and weeks spent in a casino were the best possible use of his time. I'm sure if I sat there and let him make his argument, he might even convince me. Juries let guilty men go free all the time.

Then Gunnar dropped the bombshell. It was a bombshell I didn't even know about.

"Mom's taking us back to Sweden," he said. "She's taking us there for good."

Although the news shocked me, I have to say I wasn't surprised. Apparently neither was Mr. Ümlaut. He waved his hand as if shooing away a swarm of gnats. "She's bluffing," he said. "She's been saying that forever. She'll never do it."

"This time she means it," Kjersten said. "She has airplane tickets for all of us," and then she added, "All of us but you."

This hit Mr. Ümlaut harder than anything else that had been said today. He looked at them, then looked at me as if I was somehow the mastermind of some conspiracy against him. He went away in his own head for a few moments. I could almost hear the conversation he was having with himself. Finally he spoke with the kind of conviction we had all been hoping to hear.

"She can't do that." He shook his head. "She can't legally do that. She can't just take you from the country without my permission!"

We all waited for him to make that momentous decision to DO something. Anything. This is what Gunnar and Kjersten wanted. Sure, it wasn't reconciliation between their parents, but it was the next best thing—they wanted their father to see what he was losing, and finally choose to do something about it.

I felt sure Gunnar and Kjersten had finally broken through that wall. Until Mr. Ümlaut released a long, slow sigh.

"Perhaps it's all for the best," he said. "Have your mother call me. I'll sign all the necessary papers."

And it was over. Just like that, it was over.

There are some things I don't understand, and don't think I ever will. I don't understand how a person can give up so totally and completely that they dive right into the heart of a black hole. I can't understand how someone's need to gamble, or to drink, or to shoot up, or to do anything can be greater than their need to survive. And I don't understand how pride can be more important than love.

"Our father's a proud man," Kjersten said as we drove away from the casino—as if pride can be an excuse for acting so shamefully—and yes, I know the man was sick, just as Gunnar said, but that didn't excuse the choice he made today.

I felt partially to blame, because I was the one who convinced Gunnar and Kjersten to come. I honestly believed it would make a difference. Like I said, I come from a family of fixers—but what happens when something simply can't be fixed?

I thought about my own father, fighting for his life, and winning, even as Mr. Ümlaut threw his life away, surrendering—and it occurred to me how a roll of the dice had given me back my father, and had taken theirs away.

The day was bright and sunny as we drove home, Gunnar in the back, me shotgun beside Kjersten. I wished it wasn't such a nice day out. I wished it was raining, because the mind-numbing sound of the windshield wipers swiping back and forth would have been better than the silence, or all the false emotions of the radio, which had been on for a whole minute before Kjersten turned it off. Kjersten looked a little tired, a little grateful, and a little embarrassed that I had seen their seedy family moment. It made driving home now all the more awkward.

A lot of things made more and more sense now. Gunnar's illness, for one. I wondered when he first began suspecting they might move out of the country. But being sick—that would change everything, wouldn't it? It could keep his parents together—force his father to spend money on treatment instead of gambling it away. And since the best treatment was right here in New York, no one would be going anywhere. If I were Gunnar, I might wish I had Pulmonary Monoxic Systemia, too. Because the sickness of the son might cure the sickness of the father.

I held off filling our driving silence as long as I could, but there's only so long you can resist your own nature.

"I had this friend once," I told them. "Funny kind of kid. The thing is, his mom abandoned him in a shopping cart when he was five—and his dad treated him like he didn't even exist . . ."

"So, do all your friends have screwed-up families?" Gunnar asked.

"Yeah, I'm like flypaper for dysfunction. Anyway, he had it rough for a while, did some really stupid things—but in the end he turned out okay. He even tracked down his mom."

"And they lived happily ever after?" said Gunnar.

"Well, last I heard, they both disappeared in the Bermuda Triangle—but for them that was normal."

"I think what Antsy's saying," said Kjersten, sounding a little more relaxed than she did before, "is that we're going to be fine."

"Fine might be pushing it," I said. "I would go with 'less screwed up than most people.'" That made Gunnar laugh—which was good. It meant I was getting through to him. "Who knows," I said, "maybe your dad will turn himself around someday, and you'll hear his wooden shoes walking up to your door."

"Wooden shoes are from Holland, not Sweden," Gunnar said, but I think he got the point. "And even if he does come around, who says I will?"

"You will," I told him.

"I don't think so," he said bitterly.

"Yeah, you will," I told him again. "Because you're not him."

Gunnar snarled at me, because he knew I had him. "Now you sound like my mother," he said.

"No, it's much worse than that," I told him. "I sound like *my* mother."

The fact is, Gunnar and his father might have been a lot alike—embracing their own doom, whether it was real or imagined. But in the end, Gunnar stopped carving his own tombstone. In my book, that made him twice the man his father was.

Life Is Cheap,
but Mine Is Worth More
Than a Buck Ninety-eight
in a Free-Market Economy

20 On Monday I finally listened to my phone messages—they were all back from the night we first went to the hospital, because my voice mail maxed out in just a couple of hours. The messages were all pretty much the same; people wondering how my father was, wondering how I was, and wanting to talk. The wanting-to-talk part always sounded urgent, suggesting something that was, at least in their worlds, of major importance.

And so on Monday I finally went back to school for the first time since Black Wednesday, ready to take care of business.

At first people slapped me on the back, offered their support, and all that. I wondered who would be the first to say what was really on his or her mind. I should have guessed that Wailing Woody Wilson would be the first to cross the line of scrimmage, and go deep.

"Hey, Antsy, I'm glad your dad's okay and all—but there's

something I need to talk about." The awkward look of shame in his eyes almost made me feel bad for him. "About those months I gave Gunnar. I know it was just symbolic and all, but I'd feel a whole lot better if I could have them back. Now."

"Can't do that," I said, "but how about this?" Then I pulled a notebook out of my backpack, snapped open the clasp and handed him two fresh contracts, which I had already signed. "That's two months of *my* life," I told him. "An even trade for the ones you gave Gunnar. All you have to do is sign as witness, and they're yours."

He looked at them, considered it, and said, "I guess that works," and he left.

It was like that with everybody. Even easier with some. Sometimes people never got past "Listen, Antsy—" before I handed them a month, told them *vaya con Dios,* which is like French or something for "go with God," and sent them on their merry way.

I witnessed the true nature of human greed that day, because everyone seemed to be on the dole. Once people realized what I was doing, it became a feeding frenzy. Suddenly everyone claimed to have given multiple months, even people who never gave at all. But I didn't care. I was willing to go the distance.

By the time the bell rang, ending the school day, the feeding frenzy was over, and I had given away 123 years of my life. I told Frankie this when I got to the hospital that afternoon. I thought he'd call me an idiot like he always does, but instead he was very impressed.

"You had an Initial Public Offering!" he told me. Frankie, who was on the fast track to being a stockbroker, knew all about these things. "A successful IPO means that people believe your life is worth a lot more than it actually is." And then he added, "You'd better live up to expectations, though, otherwise you go bankrupt and gotta file chapter eleven."

And since chapter eleven was pretty annoying, I'd just as soon avoid it.

Of all the conversations I had that day, the most interesting was with Skaterdud, who was skating up and down my street when I got home from school. As it turns out, things were not well in the world of Dud.

"Bad news, Antsy. I'm reeling from the blow, man, reeling. I knew I had to talk to you, because not everyone couldn't understand like you, hear me?"

"So what happened?"

"The fortune-teller—the one who told me about my burial at sea. Turns out she was a fake! Wasn't even psychic. She's been ripping people off, and telling them stuff she just made up. Got arrested for it. She didn't even have no fortune-telling license!"

"Imagine that," I said, trying to hide my smirk. "A fortune-teller making stuff up."

"You know what this means, right? It means that all bets are off. There ain't no telling when I do the root rhumba. It's all free fall without a parachute until I meet the mud. Very disturbing, dude. Very disturbing. I could get hit by a bus tomorrow."

"You probably won't."

"But I could, that's the thing. Now I gotta restructure my whole way of thinking around a world of uncertainty. I ain't none too unhappy about this."

I thought I knew where Skaterdud was leading me, but with the Dud, conversational kickflips are not uncommon, and directions can suddenly change. "So I guess you want your year back, right?"

He looked at me like I had just arrived from someone else's conversation. "No—why would I want that?"

"The same reason everybody else does," I told him. "My dad's heart attack suddenly made you all superstitious, and you're afraid you're going to lose all that time."

He shook his head. "That's just stupid." He put a scabby hand on my shoulder as we walked, as if he was an older, smarter brother imparting deep wisdom. "Here's the way I see it: that fortune-teller's a crook, right? Tried and convicted. And in a court of law when someone is guilty of theft, they usually gotta pay damages to the plaintiff, right? And is there not justice in the Universe?"

"Probably, yeah."

"So there you go." And he tapped me on the forehead to indicate the passage of knowledge into my brain.

"Uh . . . I lost you."

He threw up his hands. "Haven't you been listening? That year will come from the *fortune-teller's* life, not mine. Damages, see? She pays cosmic, karmic damages. Simple as that."

In this world, there is a fine line between enlightenment and brain damage, and I have to say that Skaterdud grinds that line perfectly balanced.

We'll Always Have *Paris, Capisce?*

21 The Saturday before their flight, the Ümlauts had a garage sale. It was more than a garage sale, though, since official foreclosure was three days away, and everything had to go before the bank took possession of the house. Most of what they owned was either on the driveway or on the dead front lawn. The rest was in the process of being carried out. I added my muscle to the effort until everything that could fit through the front door was outside in the chilly morning.

They had advertised the sale in the paper, so scavengers from every unwashed corner of Brooklyn had crawled out from under one rock or another to pick through their belongings. No question that there were deals to be made that day.

Gunnar seemed less interested in the sale than he did talking about what lay ahead.

"We'll be staying with my grandma," he told me. "At least for a while. She's got this estate outside of Stockholm."

"It's not an estate," said Kjersten. "It's just a house."

"Yeah, well, if it was here, it would be considered an estate. She even paid for our plane tickets. We're flying first class."

"Business," corrected Kjersten.

"On Scandinavian Airlines, that's just as good."

That's when I realized that somewhere between yesterday and today, Gunnar had already made the move without anyone noticing. His head was already there at that Swedish estate, settling in. Getting the rest of him there was now just a shipping expense. I marveled that in spite of everything, Gunnar was bouncing back. Suddenly he was looking forward to something other than dying. He wasn't even wearing black anymore.

I helped Kjersten sort through things in her room, which felt kind of weird, but she wanted me to be there. I'll admit I wanted to be there, too. Not so much for the sorting, but just for the being. I tried not to think about how quickly the day was moving, and how soon she'd be heading out to the airport.

"There's a two-suitcase limit per person on the flight to Stockholm," Kjersten told me. "After that, there's an extra charge." She thought about it and said, "I think I might have trouble filling both suitcases."

I guess once you start parting with all the things you think hold your life together, it's hard to stop—and then you find out your life holds together all by itself.

"It's just stuff," I told her. "And stuff is just stuff."

"Brilliant," Gunnar said from the next room. "Can I quote you on that?"

Later in the day Mr. Ümlaut came by with a U-Haul to take

away what few things didn't sell, which wasn't much, and to say his good-byes.

It was cordial, and it was awkward, but at least it happened. A ray of hope for the danglers.

"He says he's got an apartment in Queens," Gunnar told me after he left—which I suppose was a giant step up from a room at a casino—so maybe our little visit did have some effect after all. "He says he's looking for a job. We'll see."

Later that day I got a call from Mr. Crawley demanding that I come to *Paris, Capisce?* I hadn't been there since my father's heart attack. Neither had my dad—he was still at home recuperating, and leaving restaurant business to everyone else, under threat of brain surgery by my mom.

"You will report at six o'clock sharp," Crawley said. "Tell no one."

Which of course was like an invitation to tell everyone. In the end, I only told Kjersten, and asked her to come with.

"For our final date, I'm taking you to a fancy restaurant," I told her. "And this time no one's grounded."

When we arrived, I discovered, to my absolute horror, that Crawley had installed something new to complement the ambience. On the restaurant's most visible wall was a giant framed poster of me pouring water over Senator Boswell's head. There was a caption above it. It read:

PARIS, CAPISCE?
French attitude, with a hot Italian temper.

It just made Kjersten laugh, and laugh and laugh. I tried to tell myself this was a good thing—that she needed to laugh far more than I needed, oh, say self-respect?

Wonder of wonders, Crawley was actually there—in fact, I found out he had been there on a regular basis, training the staff, through various forms of employer abuse, in how to run a top-notch restaurant. When it came to the poster of me and my victim, he was very pleased with himself. "I also rented several billboards around the city," he told me.

"Where?" Kjersten wanted to know. I was a little too numb to hear the answer.

"Are we done yet?" I asked Crawley. "Can we eat now?"

"Oh," said Crawley, "but the festivities are just beginning."

Waiting in the restaurant's second room was a film crew from *Entertainment Right Now,* a daily show that featured movie news and celebrities doing scandalous things. Today's celebrity in question was none other than—yes, you guessed it—Jaxon Beale, lead singer of NeuroToxin. He sat relaxing at a table with a plate of fake food in front of him. He looked shorter than he does in music videos.

Kjersten was instantaneously starstruck, and suddenly what began as humiliation became something else entirely. "You knew all about this, didn't you!" she said to me.

I neither confirmed nor denied it. Today I was getting more mileage from silence than from ignorance.

I wasn't quite sure what this was all about, or why Crawley had requested my presence, except to maybe show off the fact that he somehow dragged a celebrity in through our doors . . .

but then someone bodily grabs me, puts me in my white bus-boy apron, and someone else puts a pitcher of water into my hands. I stood there looking dumb, one episode behind the program.

"Roll camera," the director shouts, and Jaxon looks at me, doing the bring-it-on gesture with his fingers.

"C'mon, what are you waiting for? Do I get an official welcome, or not?"

I can see Crawley grinning and wringing his fingers in anticipation in the background like Wile E. Coyote, and I finally get it. So does Kjersten.

"Omigosh!" says Kjersten. "You're going to dump water on JAXON BEALE!"

It's the first time I ever heard Kjersten, star of the debate team, say "Omigosh." All at once I realized that, for this wet, shining moment, our roles were truly reversed. Not only was I Mr. Mature, but now she was the goofy fourteen-year-old.

"Well," I said, smooth as a Porsche on ice, "if my buddy Jaxon wants water, then water he shall have." I strode up to him as Kjersten squealed with her hands over her mouth, and I said, "Welcome to *Paris, Capisce?*, Mr. Beale." Then I emptied the pitcher over his head.

He stood up, shaking the water off, and for a second I'm worried that maybe he'll get mad and punch me out, but instead, he just starts laughing, turns to the camera, and says, "Now, *that's* celebrity treatment!"

From here, I didn't need a road map to know exactly where this was leading and why. Crawley had paid Beale a small fortune for this publicity stunt, and it was money well spent. Say what you want about Creepy Crawley, but the man is a marketing genius.

"It's all about spin," Old Man Crawley said while Jaxon Beale signed a waterlogged autograph for Kjersten, and other arriving guests. "There are lots of egos out there. Once this piece airs, celebrities, politicians, you name it, will be climbing over one another to get drenched by you."

Thanks to our celebrity encounter, it became a date to remember. Even more special, because I knew it would be our last. I tried not to dwell on that, though, because we'd shared enough sad occasions together. We deserved for this one to be happy. I ordered in Italian—I don't speak it all that well, but I can order like a pro. Still on her Jaxon Beale high, Kjersten was all gush, flush, and blush for a while. "I probably looked so stupid!" she said. "Like one of those lame adoring fans."

"Naa," I told her. "You're cute when you're embarrassed."

By the time dessert came, everything settled down, and the dating balance was restored. It was different now, though. For the first time, I felt more like her equal. Maybe now she saw me that way, too—and it occurred to me that a relationship isn't about being two distinct kinds of people—it's about feeling comfortable in whatever roles the moment required.

I guess that's why my friendship with Lexie survived through Norse gods and echolocation—we always seemed to be what the other one needed.

"Tell you what," Lexie told me as we sat in her living room one afternoon, planning her grandfather's next kidnapping. "If we both happen to be in between relationships, I see nothing wrong with going out to dinner, or a concert now and then."

I think it was good for both of us to know that as long as we were both there for each other, we'd always have a social life, even when we had no social life.

On the morning of the Ümlauts' flight to Sweden, we had a funeral.

I'd like to say it was symbolic, but, sadly, it was all too real. Ichabod, our beloved family cat, finally went to the great windowsill in the sky. We decided to bury him in the Ümlauts' backyard, since there was already a sizable gravestone available that otherwise would have gone to waste. Gunnar spackled over his own name, then chiseled out ICHABOD on the other side, and it was good to go.

Christina had written a heartfelt eulogy that I suspect she had been working on for months, the way newspapers start preparing obituaries the instant a celebrity gets a hangnail. With all the family pictures covering the little wooden crate, and the solemn air of the occasion, Ichabod's memorial service actually brought a few tears to my eyes. I didn't mind that Kjersten and Gunnar saw me cry over a cat. After everything I'd been through, I had a right. And realistically, who would they tell in Sweden?

With Ichabod laid to rest, we went inside to find Mrs. Ümlaut sweeping the empty kitchen, because "I don't want the bank to think we're slobs."

"She's just like our mother," Christina noted. I think all mothers are alike, regardless of cultural background, when it comes to illogical cleaning.

Christina wanted to go home and mourn privately, but I made her wait, because I wanted to see Kjersten and Gunnar off. The luggage was at the front door, waiting for the arrival of the taxi. Six pieces, and a couple of carry-ons.

Gunnar looked at his house with no outward show of emotion. "We had mice," he said. "And the drains never smelled right. It's just as well." I'm sure he felt a lot more than he let on, but it was his way. Kjersten, on the other hand, had moist eyes all over the place. Every corner seemed to hold a hidden memory. She looked fondly into empty places while Mrs. Ümlaut kept going around the house, up and down the stairs.

"There's something I forgot," she kept saying. "I know there's something I forgot."

Eventually Kjersten gently grabbed her, and gave her a hug to slow her down. "Everything's taken care of, Mom. Everything's ready." The two rocked back and forth for a moment, and I couldn't tell whether Mrs. Ümlaut was rocking her baby girl, or if Kjersten was rocking her anxious mother. Kjersten grinned at me over her mother's shoulder, and I offered her an understanding smile back.

There's no question I was going to miss Kjersten, but the kind of sadness I felt wasn't the kind that brings up tears, and I'm thinking, *Great, I cried for the cat, but I'm not crying for her*—but I think she was okay with that.

I think we both knew if she stayed, our relationship wouldn't have gone much further. Ours was like one of those fireplace Duraflame logs that burns big and bright, then drops dead an hour before the package says it will. I think it's best that we left it here, before it became useless.

"So," I asked her, only half joking, "once you get there, do you think you'll start dating guys your own age?"

She looked at me with a grin, then looked away. "Antsy, I think you've aged at least two years over the past few weeks," she told me. "No matter what, you're going to be a hard act to follow."

For that, I gave her the best kiss of my career—during which Christina said, "Oh! Is that why you brushed your teeth this morning?"

The taxi finally arrived, honking from outside in repeated little blasts like a fire drill. Gunnar and I brought the luggage to the cabdriver, who, like every New York cabdriver, acted like it was an insult to his profession that he had to load luggage.

Thanks to all the horn blasts, neighbors had come out onto their porches to watch the Ümlauts' departure. Then Mrs. Ümlaut threw up her hands "Ah! Now I remember!" She ran back into the house and came out with something in her hand. "This is for you," she said to me. "Someone wanted to buy it last Saturday, but I told them it wasn't for sale."

She handed me the stainless-steel meat tenderizer.

"To remember us by," she said with a wink.

This was the first hint that she had a sense of humor—and a twisted one, too. I was impressed.

"It'll be one of my prized possessions—I'll keep it with my rare paper clips," I told her, and she looked at me funny. "No, really."

"You must visit us!" she said, which I figured was about as likely as me visiting the International Space Station, but I nodded politely and said, "Sure."

Then I heard a gruff voice from somewhere down the block intrude on our tender farewell moment.

"What about our plants, hah?" I turned to see the same paunchy, beady-eyed man, who had made nasty comments before, peering down from his second-floor balcony. From this angle, the guy looked like what you might get if you crossed a human being with one of those potbellied pigs. "You gonna send us back some freakin' tulips?" he mocked.

Mrs. Ümlaut sighed, and Kjersten shook her head as she got into the taxi. "Why does everyone confuse us with Holland?"

"I know this guy," says Christina. "His kid's in my class. He eats pencil sharpenings."

"Go on," grunted the pig-man. "Get atta here! We don't need ya!"

I'm about to tell the guy off—but then I hear a bang, and I see that Gunnar has jumped up on the trunk of the taxi—and, to the driver's extreme chagrin, Gunnar climbs up so he's standing on the taxi's roof.

"You can't get rid of me!" he yells to the pig-man. Then he turns to address all the neighbors, speaking loud and clear: "I'll be everywhere—wherever you look. Wherever there's a fight so hungry people can eat, I'll be there. Wherever they's a cop beatin' up a guy, I'll be there. I'll be in the way guys yell when they're mad, an' I'll be in the way kids laugh when they're hungry an' they know supper's ready. An' when our folks eat the stuff they raise an' live in the houses they build—why, I'll be there."

I had to smile—I even applauded, because at last Gunnar had found a real quote. And with all due respect to John Steinbeck, as far as I'm concerned, Gunnar owns it now!

Gunnar took a long, elaborate bow, then hopped down from the roof, and did something very un-Gunnar-like. He gave me this sudden, death-grip hug that crunched my bones like a chiropractor. When he let go, we stood there for a moment, feeling stupid.

"Dewey Lopez didn't get a picture of that, did he?" I asked.

"If he did, it's your problem now." Then he jumped in the taxi. "Ciao."

Kjersten put her hand out the window for one final farewell grasp, and the taxi driver floored it, nearly leaving Kjersten's hand behind with me. I watched as they accelerated down the street and turned the corner.

"Someday," said Christina, "I hope to have friends as problematic as yours."

My thoughts were still on Kjersten. I wish I could have come up with a quote like Gunnar did—y'know, the absolute perfect parting words to leave Kjersten with.

But what do you say to a Scandinavian beauty who's about to get on a plane and fly out of your life?

A Weed Grows in Brooklyn

22 Just as Old Man Crawley predicted, *Paris, Capisce?* had celebrities dragging their nails over one another's backs to get in the door. We ended up having to schedule celebrities—one per night—so they didn't all arrive at once. Dad, still recuperating, took the calls from home, chatting with agents, and the stars themselves. It was great! I got to meet more famous people than I thought I'd meet in a lifetime, then pour water over their heads.

With all this celebrity appeal, the restaurant was packed every night with people hoping to eat a fine meal, spot someone famous, and see them get drenched—either by me, or this guy they hired who looked and sounded like me, which I still find too creepy to talk about.

Christina even got into it, selling the pitchers we used on eBay for prices that could fund her college education someday.

Long story short, by the time Dad was ready to go back to

work, *Paris, Capisce?* was the hottest restaurant in Brooklyn. We were all realistic enough to know that trends pass, that it wouldn't last forever, but we'd also been through enough to know we gotta enjoy what we got, when we got it.

"It's gonna be different now," he told us. "Now that the restaurant's always busy, there's going to be a lot more work."

So he doubled his staff, and cut his own hours in half, leaving the stress for someone else. He even has time to cook at home with Mom again, and watch a game or two on the weekends with me.

"When I finally go, I'm sure it'll be a heart attack," he said to me. "But let's hope I go like your grandpa"—whose ticker didn't give out until he was pushing eighty-eight.

It's all about spin, Old Man Crawley had said. Spin makes a big difference, doesn't it? My father almost died, but spin it a little, and it's a life-changing warning that taught him to appreciate the important things in life. And the Ümlauts—they lost just about everything they had, but with the right spin, it becomes a shining opportunity to start fresh.

I went back to their block a few months later, out of curiosity more than anything else. The house was still empty, and still at the center of a dust bowl. The bank that now owned the home was still trying to find a buyer—but, see, my sister, in her attempt to keep Ichabod undisturbed, had started a rumor that the backyard didn't just contain a single cat grave—it was, in fact, a local pet cemetery, and the final resting place of a hundred neighborhood critters—not all of them resting in peace.

Funny thing about rumors, the harder a rumor is to believe,

the more likely it's going to chase buyers away. Serves the bank right.

As I approached the house that day, I saw a single weed trying to poke its way up through a crack in the pavement. The first sign that the dust bowl was over! Then, as I looked more closely at the yards all around me, I could see patches of little ugly weeds popping up everywhere. Life was coming back to the street, and I thought how appropriate that the first plants to come back will be the plants all the neighbors will kill with more herbicide. Thus is the cycle of life.

Me, I had better things to do than watch the weeds grow—because for my fifteenth birthday, my parents got me a passport, and a plane ticket. Brooklyn weeds may have their own unique charm—but I hear spring break is beautiful in Sweden!

APPENDIX 1

More Fake Quotes by Gunnar Ümlaut

"A family is a collection of strangers trapped in a web of DNA and forced to cope." —Maria von Trapp

"No luncheon shall ever present itself free from payment in coin or pound of flesh." —William Shakespeare

"All right, I admit to having cursed the darkness once or twice." —Eleanor Roosevelt

"Being rich is nothing when compared to being really, really rich." —Bill Gates

"What no one seems to realize is that there are no bathrooms on the moon." —Neil Armstrong

"I do not mourn the loss of my hearing, and in fact, I foresee a time when popular music shall cause entire populations to long for my affliction." —Ludwig van Beethoven

"Time is the unquantifiable commodity that greases the gear work of creation. But I prefer Russian dressing." —Albert Einstein

"The fabrication of quotes is like the manufacture of polyester. It may pretend to be silk, but suffocates when the climate is hot." —Mahatma Gandhi

APPENDIX 2

The Death Euphemisms of Skaterdud

Pushing Posies

Meeting the Mud

The Dirt Dance

Snooze Button Bingo

The Root Rhumba

Sucking Seaweed*

The Formaldehyde High

Visiting Uncle Mort

Sniffing Satin

The China Express

Bucket Soccer

The Last Lawn Party

Farm Finale

The Shovel Symphony

Chillin' with Jimi

Box Potato

El Sayonara Grande

---

*For burial at sea.

APPENDIX 3

Antsy Bonano's Time Contract
(in its final version)

I, _____ being of sound mind and body, do hereby bequeath one month of my natural life to Gunnar Ümlaut, subject to the stuff listed below:

1. The month shall not be this coming May or June, or the last month of Gunnar Ümlaut's life, any leap-year Februaries, or the months of his high school or college graduations, or the month of his marriage, should he live to those dates, as those months are already reserved by others.

2. The month shall be taken from the end of my natural life, and not the middle.

3. The donated month shall be null and void if my own expiration date is less than 31 days from the date of this contract, regardless of the length of the month which is ultimately donated.

4. Should Gunnar Ümlaut use my month for criminal acts such as shoplifting or serial killing, I shall not be held responsible.

5. The month shall be reduced to two weeks should Gunnar Ümlaut become my enemy for any reason including but not limited to the following: familial feud, personal grudge, nonrepayment of debt, all forms of bad-mouthing, hallway bullying, refusing a reasonable request to share lunch.

6. Gunnar Ümlaut, and/or his next of kin shall have no claim on property, or chunks of time beyond those granted in this contract, and said month shall have no cash value, unless mutually agreed upon, in which case I shall share equally in the cash value, without limitation, with the exception of limitations rising from the verifiable end of Gunnar Ümlaut's life, either prior to or after aforementioned end.

7. Should any disputes arise from the exchange of this month, both parties agree to submit to binding arbitration by Anthony Bonano, who in this contract shall be known as the Master of Time.

_____

Signature

_____

Signature of Witness